The Wifey I Used to Be 2

Lock Down Publications and
Ca$h Presents

The Wifey I Used to Be 2

A Novel by Nicole Goosby

Lock Down Publications
P.O. Box 944
Stockbridge, Ga 30281

Visit our website
www.lockdownpublications.com

First Edition March 2021
Printed in the United States of America

Lock Down Publications
Like our page on Facebook: Lock Down Publications @
www.facebook.com/lockdownpublications.ldp
Cover design and layout by: **Dynasty Cover Me**
Book interior design by: **Shawn Walker**
Editor: **Tamira Butler**

Stay Connected with Us!

Text **LOCKDOWN** to 22828 to stay up-to-date with new releases, sneak peaks, contests and more…
Thank you.

Submission Guideline.

Submit the first three chapters of your completed manuscript to ldpsubmissions@gmail.com, subject line: Your book's title. The manuscript must be in a .doc file and sent as an attachment. Document should be in Times New Roman, double spaced and in size 12 font. Also, provide your synopsis and full contact information. If sending multiple submissions, they must each be in a separate email.

Have a story but no way to send it electronically? You can still submit to LDP/Ca$h Presents. Send in the first three chapters, written or typed, of your completed manuscript to:

LDP: Submissions Dept
P.O. Box 944
Stockbridge, Ga 30281

DO NOT send original manuscript. Must be a duplicate.

Provide your synopsis and a cover letter containing your full contact information.

Thanks for considering LDP and Ca$h Presents.

Prologue

Shoney

Okay, okay, now where was I? Oh, yeah—I was telling y'all about Raylon's no-good ass. Well, for me to sit here and scream some shit about how everything was going great and how life was good would be a damn lie, and the furthest thing from the truth. Not only had some shit changed concerning Raylon and the way we were living, but I'd changed, and I mean that literally.

It'd been around eight months since I'd last gotten to tell y'all about some of the things I'd been dealing with, but believe me when I tell you, the shit was crazier now.

As you've figured by now, my man wasn't the one that came to bail me out of that hell hole. Matter of fact, it was days later when I even heard from his ass. He'd fucked around and gotten jammed up himself—and let him tell it—if it wasn't for my arrest, he wouldn't have been caught with over ten ounces of heroin while entering another state. Yeah, I was fucked up about it at first, but I eventually said fuck it—I'd been blamed for shit before.

Besides, the picture he'd painted me of us still had its color. And like always, I was the bitch he called to save his ass, and like many of the times before—I did. Only thing was that this time, I didn't have income tax money to turn over, or even a stash of my own to pay for bail and an attorney. I did something fucked up to get his case dismissed, and when I say fucked up, I'm talking about bad—but I'll get to that later.

Yeah, yeah, I know y'all cursing a bitch out, but let me finish. I had a plan. Well, September and I had a plan—and to see it through, we needed my man. My husband. Yep, Raylon and I got married five months ago and had been living together for the past six. I told y'all the shit was crazy, but anyway, money was being spent and made again—if you know what I mean. Not only was I wifey now, but he'd moved me into a nice two-story house not too far from where Sept and I lived.

I still dropped by my old spot as often as I could 'cause that was now our headquarters, according to Sept. But for the most part, I was on my big girl shit for real, for real. Since my cosmetic procedure, I'd lost sixty-three pounds, and a bitch couldn't tell me shit. I'm not going to lie and say I was no damn Barbie, or anywhere near September's build, but I was nice. I reminded you of one of them chocolate bunnies niggas ran to get their girls when they'd fucked up and wanted to be forgiven.

Yeah, my ass and thighs were firmer, stomach smaller, titties down a couple of cups, and if I were to believe Raylon's lying ass, my pussy had gotten smaller and tighter also, but he loved it. I mean, that nigga's dick stayed hard when he got around me. My girl even tried to convince me to submit some pics to one of them *Plush XL* magazines for money because a bitch was looking both print and poster worthy for real now. I still worked the same job, along with September's crazy ass. I still worked out, and we were still doing the keto dieting thing.

As expected, weight fell off of me after the first month. I'd changed my way of living to a certain extent. I guess there was some good in all this, but I was still putting up with a nigga that felt as if I could be given sugar and treated like shit. I mean, Raylon laced me with money and nice things, fucked me like I needed and wanted to be, but the nigga still cheated. It was no loving, but I had to do what I had to do—at least for now, anyway.

My closet wasn't like September's yet, but my shit was noteworthy. I could step out in a $5,000 outfit on any given day. I now drove a CLS on a daily, had a 2017 Tacoma truck in the garage, and was promised a BMW M6 coupe I had to have. There were things I expected regularly, and there were things I feigned surprise when receiving—like the Caiman Gator Louis Vuitton bag and matching peep-toe heels Raylon bought me yesterday.

He and Daxx had moved in on some guy's turf, and money was coming in from everywhere it seemed. And instead of asking a shit load of questions and being lied to, I just played my position and let them be. All I knew was that I wouldn't be the one trafficking any drugs anymore, nor was Raylon allowed to drive either of my automobiles, 'cause I was not about to go through that jail shit again.

Now, Brent was another story altogether. That nigga went from working in a barber shop to owning a used car lot and detail shop in under a year. I tried to tell Sept that something wasn't right with either of them, but she only regarded me with twisted lips, a blank stare, and silence. Obviously, she didn't give a damn. But, hey, let me go and feed this nigga some of this pussy, because he'd been screaming my name for the past twenty minutes, and the least I could do was send him on his way with a full stomach, a limp dick, and a smile.

As soon as I finished with him, got me a couple of hours in at the gym, and checked in with September's crazy ass, I'm going to sit down and tell y'all the rest of my story. And for those of you that think you've got it all figured out? Believe me—you don't. And for all of you motherfuckers that's still getting dragged by your so-called "hubbies" and ain't got shit to show for it? Grab ya towels and get ready to soak this shit up, 'cause I'm about to spill tea.

Herbal tea, at that.

Enjoy.

Chapter One

Shoney

For the past few months, I'd been debating whether or not to quit my job because it was always some drama, and truth be told, I still didn't trust Sept working there alone. The idea of being able to stay home chillaxing with a colander of seedless grapes, out on my patio reading, or at the gym breaking a nice sweat stayed at the forefront of my mind, but I'd allowed Sept to convince me to stay a little while longer. Let her tell it, it was a part of the plan. But today had started out as one of the many others that gave me more than enough reason to walk out.

I'd been at my station filing a stack of forms for twenty minutes—I mean, twenty good, quiet minutes—before I heard September's voice from the cubicle across the way. Instead of her helping the woman apply for assistance, job training, and some of the other programs we had to offer, she was going off on her for having kids by niggas that couldn't care less, and was admonishing her for trying to cuff her kids' fathers with child support. I, at first, just glanced in that general direction, because it always seemed that September got a little loud, and at times vulgar, but when seeing several other co-workers head in that direction, I stood.

"God dammit, Sept!"

She was now standing inches in front of the teary-eyed woman with her finger in her face, and they looked as if they were about to come to blows. As always, people crowded just to stand and watch, and I had to push my way through the crowd.

"Excuse me! Excuse—Sept, what the fuck is going on now?!" I yelled before stepping in between them.

"Man, fuck this bitch, Shoney. I'm trying to give the bitch some game, but she'd rather crawl up in here every month begging for more WIC, and stamps, and this other bullshit."

I looked from September to the woman—younger woman, I might add—and something pulled at my heart. There was no doubt Sept had struck a couple of nerves by putting her on blast and airing all of her laundry, but still. Pride was a bitch that I gave a damn about, and there were other ways to address her.

"Come with me, sweetheart." I bent down, grabbed her purse, and pushed her towards my station. "Both of y'all need to chill out."

"She just started off calling me all kinds of dumb bitches and shit. She doesn't know me like that," the young woman cried.

After leading her away from the fray and pushing her past onlookers, I told her to sit in my seat while I took up the chair in front of my desk. I looked at her, offered her a napkin, and reached for one myself. "You good now?"

She and I talked for the next forty minutes about some of everything, but instead of being the one that *talked at her*, I listened, offered her a different perspective, and let her know that she wasn't the only woman going through what she was. I understood exactly where she was at in her life. I'd been there, stayed, looked for every reason to leave, and still couldn't.

By the time she left, I'd given her a little more than she should have received, as well as my number, because hers was a story I had to follow up on.

I was stuck in thoughts of my own when I heard a loud bang on my cubicle desk. I could feel the smile I wore fade as I looked up to see my girl, Sept, looking down at me. She then replaced the stapler she'd used to snatch me from my thoughts.

"What the hell you over here smiling for, freak?"

I looked around to see who else might have been watching me, and told her, "I'm just over here thinking, is all."

"The way you and that stupid bitch was over here laughing it up, I could have sworn y'all were long-lost friends or something."

"Ouu, bitch—jealousy wears Jimmy Choo now?" I looked past Sept while straightening up my desk. Our supervisor was approaching. It was like him to show up after the bullets found their marks. I could only roll my eyes.

"Good morning, ladies," Mr. Dillan spoke, and before I could speak, September spun around on him.

"Who ran and told it now, Mr. Dillan?" she spat.

I interrupted before another scene could be made. "I took care of it, Mr. Dillan. Everything is everything. We're good."

He smiled. Mr. Dillan told me he was thankful for my help, because we all knew he couldn't handle September, and the only reason he was here now was because someone had ran and told him of another one of her altercations. I returned a smile and nodded—what was understood didn't have to be voiced.

As soon as he turned to leave, Sept turned back to me as if nothing ever happened.

"With his punk ass."

I didn't know what it was she had on the man, but whatever it was, it had him looking past the shit she did, said, and even the write-ups he threatened her with. Me, personally, I would have fired her ass, but then again, she'd more than likely have some shit on me too. That was the way she played the game.

***

Brent

After texting September for the third time, and returning the "thumbs up" to Raylon, I slid my phone into my pocket and made my way towards the surface area of the compound. I'd recently rented a transporter and wanted to make sure things were in order for the six automobiles I'd just purchased. Things had been happening so fast for the past few months, and it was either get in front of it, or get ran over by it, and I was continually on the go. If I wasn't at the banks with Sheila, I was perusing through a selection of cars and trucks being auctioned, or at the detail shop overseeing renovations. Yeah, I was busy as shit, but making money demanded that.

This was the fourth police auction I'd attended, and the first time I'd finally seen the car I'd been looking for, for damn near a year now. The only thing was that I wanted to at least speak with Sept and let her know that I was about to buy her the Lexus, but instead of the convertible she wanted, it was a coupe. I promised her I'd be on the lookout, and now that I was within reach of it, I needed her to get back at me—like yesterday.

"Yo, Brent!"

I turned around and saw the guy I'd hired to inspect the purchases, then walked towards him. "Hey, what we got?"

"Everything's good. All the automobiles checked out perfectly. Now we're just waiting for the paperwork to clear."

I smiled to myself, because those were the exact words Sheila told me they'd say. With her being our accountant now, I was able to get the big business loan for both the lot and the detail shop. She made sure funds were placed where they needed to be, and for once, it felt good as hell knowing we were putting money in the bank instead of hiding it in drawers in a closet. Sheila had us on our corporate game in a major way.

I nodded towards the black coupe and asked, "What's up with the Lexus?"

"I heard it was a new arrival. Sent along with some more confiscated luxury cars."

"I want it," I told him before heading in that direction.

"That's a brand-new car, Brent. The starting bid is going to be around thirty or forty grand."

Before I could respond to that, Raylon walked up looking as if he was scheduled for some male modeling shoot. I looked the nigga over—sure that he'd raised a few brows. The nigga wore some peach-colored linen pants, a cream-colored linen shirt, and a pair of tan leather loafers—no socks—and some gold-trimmed Cartier shades. I hated when he drew attention in places we didn't need any. I might have been running a legitimate business now, but the flip of a rock would bring both buildings down, and him rolling up looking like anything other than a nigga trying to make it would have the cops talking.

"Where we at, Big Boy?"

"We all good, homie. The ink drying as we speak," I told him while walking closer to the Lexus coupe.

He removed his glasses and smiled. “Whose shit is this?”

“I’m trying to run it down right now. Sept’s gonna love this one,” I told him, knowing his brain was in overdrive.

“Sept?” Raylon frowned before continuing. “Sept? Nigga, is you crazy? Fuck that bitch. If she wants another car, let her bitch ass buy it.”

It didn’t have to be said that he and Sept weren’t the best of friends, but she was my girl, and being that I’d already told her about my plans, I wasn’t about to let my friends talk me out of them. “Did I say anything when you started talking about buying Shoney that BMW coupe?” I then tilted my head to the side while awaiting his answer.

“Nigga, I was just saying. Shit, you knew I wasn’t about to—”

“I already got it,” I told him before he could complete his lie.

He knew he would have done and spent whatever for his wife. Hell, he’d been buying all kinds of shit for Shoney for a while now.

“You did what?” he asked.

“You heard me, nigga. We got ya wife the car she wanted, now I’m about to get my girl the one she wants.” I looked back towards the technician and told him, “Make it happen.”

It wasn’t until we’d walked off did Raylon say, “I know we making money, nigga, but damn.”

There was no need in me bringing up the fact that he’d, not too long ago, put down on a quarter-million-dollar house, bought three cars, and another truck, and was rumored to have lost over 20k at the Shack a week ago, because it would only start another argument. Daxx already gave me the rundown on what he’d done.

“Um, yeah, yeah, I was meaning to tell you that I’m going to do something else with my money. I don’t like that bitch knowing my business like that.”

And there it was. He always went there when he was doing more than he claimed to have been doing. Hell, if it wasn’t for Sheila schooling me on this shit, we wouldn’t have been about to make the moves we were making now.

I only nodded. “That’s cool.”

Not only did I have insurance on my money, but I was able to move it the way I needed to without the cops pulling me over, or niggas getting the win when they stumbled across it. I was getting all the way out of the game—we all agreed on it long before now, but that was obviously what Raylon had forgotten about.

"Yo, Brent!"

I faced the technician wearing a hopeful expression.

"Fifty grand, and you got yourself a Lexus coupe." He beamed.

I reached in my pocket for my phone and speed-dialed Sheila. "Load that bitch up before these hoes change their minds," I told him before making my way to the office.

Raylon followed.

***

Daxx

With Raylon playing house, and Brent running behind September's trifling ass, I was left to maintain our presence in the streets, as well as run our operation. Raylon was finally able to see that both my strategy and plans were far more lucrative than his so-called "point of view." Months had passed since surviving the hit Four Fingers put on us, and if it wasn't for a couple of heroin addicts like Rubberhead and Gunz, we would have all been dead.

Come to find out, not only did Fingers have a bitch loyal to him—the same bitch had been playing me like an acoustic guitar. Karen was his bottom bitch and had been for a while. To where I saw so much potential in her, her promise was to him, and once we ran up on the man himself, that's exactly where we found Karen also. Rubberhead, Gunz, and I had gotten more information than needed, just before Rubberhead slit the youngster's throat, and that was the only way we found where Fingers had been hiding both himself and his fortune.

We'd sat for two hours waiting for Fingers to show, and once he did, seeing Karen climb out of his Phantom made it all that much sweeter. It was evident that we were believed to be dead because of the expressions they both wore, and it was right before Rubberhead had his way with her did she disclose the location of the drugs and money stashed at the same house.

'Til this day, I still couldn't get the images of Karen's disfigured and swollen face out of my mind. Rubberhead had smashed the entire right side of her face with a wooden table leg and would have done more had I not stopped him. The once beautiful Karen was now a slit-throat memory because of her role in the game she played. And as for Fingers? Closed casket wasn't even necessary.

That night we left Fingers, we got away with over eleven kilos of cocaine, seven kilos of heroin, and damn near 1.2 million dollars in cash. I knew personally that half of the money was owed, but that was his problem. After giving Rubberhead and Gunz four kilos of cocaine, one kilo of heroin, and $50,000 apiece, we called it a wrap and promised to keep in touch. That was eight months ago, and despite all they were given, I was now convincing Rubberhead to make the trip to Mexico for the eight kilos Raylon was purchasing. The words of the wise were true: the more dope you gave an addict to have, the more dope you gave an addict to use.

"Why don't we just go down there and bleed they ass, Daxx? We both know them motherfuckers sitting on a hell of a lot more than what they selling ya boy, Raylon."

I shook my head in disagreement. Going up against a cartel was nothing like we'd experienced with Four Fingers and his clique of youngsters, and even that was something I wouldn't do twice.

"Business is good on our end, Rubberhead. Real good," I told him before sending the text to Raylon.

"Y'all running around here finger-fucking these hoes when what they really need is some hard dickin', Daxx. You know how this shit goes."

I watched Rubber snort a couple of lines of the winter white, saw him throw his head back, and close his eyes. The drug silenced him. "In due time, Rubberhead. In due time."

"Just point and get the fuck out of the way, Daxx. That's all you have to do," he told me before nodding off into his drug-induced slumber.

I might not have admitted it, but that had been in my thoughts for the longest. However, business was good, and of course, I didn't have a team big enough to ride against an established cartel.

Now that Fingers was out of the way, and a couple of scary asses were afraid to set-up shop, Raylon and I put a choke hold on the game and were flooding both the North and the Westside with both heroin and cocaine. And with Rubberhead and Gunz fucking off more than they could keep, we kept them on the road. We'd been looking at over 8k a month on work alone, and after splitting that million with Brent and Raylon, I still had over $600,000 to myself. By the way things were looking, it wasn't about to slow down any-time soon, and with Sheila doing her thing, money was in the bank, literally. Things were going perfect. I just had to make sure it stayed that way.

***

September

Brent's text couldn't have come at a better time, because Shoney was an anxiety attack waiting to happen. Guilt rode her like a thick bitch on a four-inch dick. I'd been coaching her for the long-est, and I wasn't about to let her fuck it all off because she was feeling guilty. Yeah, she was married now, but like I told her, it only meant she didn't have to pay the toll fee when it came to Ray-lon. No longer did she have to pay for the dick. The dick now paid her, but she was more worried about the nigga who owned the dick being faithful.

Yeah, some sad shit, for real. She was finally understanding the cards we were playing but still felt as if we'd been going too hard for too long. She now had a nice two-story home, a couple of luxury automobiles, and a noteworthy wardrobe because of him. Aside from the money—I'm talking, thousands upon thousands—he was none the wiser. For once, Shoney had her own, and I made her promise a while back that she'd ride with me until I felt it was time to stop. I personally broke myself for Shoney, and she knew it.

So, now we played to my song and dance, because I was going to break her no-good ass husband, and as agreed, she was going to help me. The thing now was that she was seeing a little money and playing a role we'd only rehearsed a time or two before the lights and cameras came on.

"I'm telling you, Sept, Raylon ain't stupid. He's been playing this game for the longest."

I looked from Shoney to the clock that hung above Mr. Dillan's office because it was almost quitting time, and I couldn't wait to show her just how stupid her nigga was. I told her, "That's just it, Shoney. The nigga been playing. He ain't used to a motherfucker playing him. Especially his wife."

"He knows me, Sept. He knows something's up."

"Will you please stop? That nigga too worried about you catching him doing something. The last thing on that nigga's mind is catching you doing anything."

I got so tired of explaining shit to her naive ass that I showed her the pics Brent sent to me. The exact ones he told me not to show her. "Here. This the type of shit my game rewards me."

"Whose car is this, September?"

I yanked my phone from her, scrolled down a lil' ways, and handed it back. "Read the text, Shoney." I watched her cover her mouth with her hand, then look up at me and back to the screen. She scrolled upward. I told her, "Just sit back and enjoy the ride. I got this."

"Oh my gosh, Sept. How—"

I, again, snatched my phone from her when seeing our co-worker, Alyssa. I knew when a bitch was trying to get an ear and an eyeful, and when seeing her slow her pace and act as if she was searching for something in the things she carried, I told my girl, "Hold on, Shoney. Let this nosey ass bitch go on about her business." I couldn't stand these broke ass hoes I worked with.

"Huh? Um, girl, ain't nobody studding you, September."

Shoney and I watched her pass, apparently finding whatever it was she was looking for. I was just about to continue the conversation I was having with Shoney, until I heard the bitch mumble something about me being a "fake ass bitch."

"Sept, don't even start. You already got one write-up today."

I turned back towards the voice and yelled, "Meet me out in the parking lot, and get a fake foot in your ass then, bitch!"

No sooner than the words came out, Mr. Dillan came walking around the corner, and Shoney stood.

"It ain't nothing, Mr. Dillan. They was just—"

I cut my girl off and asked him, "What now?"

"Um, Ms. Hassan, can you please come to my office for a sec?" he said before walking in that direction.

"Is that how long it takes for these hoes to get you off?" I said loud enough for him to turn slightly, and for Shoney to grab my arm and pull me towards her.

I was more than positive Mr. Dillan wanted to discuss things other than me going off on a bitch, but you couldn't get Shoney to understand that. Every time I was summoned to the supervisor's office, she found herself standing at the edge of some cliff thinking we'd be pushed over shortly. It might have been that after every one of my outbursts and incidents that I was called to Mr. Dillan's office, but if she only knew the half of the shit I knew, she wouldn't worry herself so much. But fuck it. There would be a time for that, but for now, I only winked at her before heading off towards our supervisor's office.

"Don't go in there showing yo' ass, September."

"The last thing Mr. Dillan wants to see is my ass, Shoney. Believe me."

Chapter Two

Shoney

I'd waited for three days for Raylon to surprise me, and it had gotten to the point where I'd begun questioning whether or not Sept knew what she was talking about. She'd been pushing her Lexus coupe ever since that first day and assured me that I'd be doing the same sooner or later, and later came later than I'd expected.

We were at the house going over "the plan" and sipping on fresh squeezed juices when Raylon finally pulled up driving the midnight blue BMW convertible with a huge blue bow on its trunk. I rolled my eyes at September because she was staring at me with her "know it all" expression, and now was not the time for one of her speeches. I slowly walked away from the window facing the driveway and made my way to where she'd just sat on the suede sectional that damn near wrapped around my sitting room.

"Play the part, Shoney. Play the motherfucking part, tramp."

I smiled, took a sip of the juice I held, and whispered over the rim of the glass, "I got this end. You just chill out, and don't start no shit." I then hit the setting on the remote to select Anita Baker's "Giving You the Best That I Got" to set the tone.

"Shoney! Shoney!"

"We're in here, babe." I gave Sept one last look, then smiled when seeing my husband appear in the doorway. "Why didn't you wake me before you left, babe?" I stood, greeted my man with a nice kiss, and let him palm my ass.

"Hey, I've got something for you, babe."

I pulled back from his embrace, looked down at the bulge in his slacks, and said, "I bet you do."

"Hey, Sept. I didn't see you over there."

"Um."

"You don't have to keep buying me stuff, Raylon. I know you love me." I smiled, knowing September must have been boiling mad hearing those words, but fuck it. He was in rare form. "Boy!" Raylon had leaned down, scooped me up into his strong arms, and spun me around. “Raylon, we have company,” I told him, knowing it was moments like this that led to him carrying me into a coatroom, or some other place where he’d strip me of my clothes and have his way.

“She good. The surprise is outside, babe. Close your eyes.”

“Outside?” I quickly complied with his order and wrapped my arms around his neck.

“No peeking, Shoney,” he told me.

“Oh, don’t worry. She—”

“Don’t drop me, Raylon. They just waxed my floors.” I had to say something because Sept didn’t need too much to light her fire. As soon as my bare feet touched the cool concrete of our driveway, Raylon stood directly in front of me to block my view.

“Shoney, you’ve been nothing but the best to me, and if it wasn’t for you, none of this would have been possible. I owe you the world, babe, and this is just a fragment of all that’s to come.”

My man looked so damn handsome when he pulled the game he owned, and had it been early in our relationship, I would have believed every bit of it, but still. I loved when he did it.

“Baby, I—” I froze a bit too soon and reacted a little too late for Sept, because now her lips were twisted, and her eyes had been rolled.

“Don’t hate,” Raylon told her when seeing the same.

“Nigga, ain’t nobody hating on your—”

I gasped louder the second time. “Raylon! When—how—” I feigned surprise, placed my hand over my chest, and allowed him to pull me towards the car. Sept followed. And just as it began, it was over. Once he’d given me the key fob, along with a folded envelope, and the promise to be home early tonight, he jumped in his truck and sped off—said something about having to meet up with Daxx.

“Pretty boy ass nigga.”

After waving him off, I turned to Sept, who then hurried to her trunk, grabbed her backpack, and headed back inside.

“I told him I was taking you shopping.” I thumbed through the bills inside of the envelope I was given.

"How much he give you?"

"Um, looks like around six grand."

Sept snatched the envelope. "Perfect. That's exactly how much I brought. Come on."

After following her inside and watching her do her thing, I tossed the key fob onto the smoked-glass nightstand and fell across my bed. I asked her, "How much longer, Sept?"

"Until I say so, Shoney. Don't start that shit, and tonight, when you're getting fucked silly, don't say shit. You just bend that ass over and play the part, you hear me?"

I nodded at her through the mirrored-ceiling of my bedroom. I laid there while she flopped down across from me. She was punching out texts with both thumbs. In her mind, she was on her best shit, and as bad as I wanted to admit it, I knew it was just a matter of time before it all came apart. Then, too, she'd been plotting on this for a minute now.

"Don't be one of the dizzy ass housewives that end up with nothing, Shoney. You tax his ass for everything you can. You're married now, so you've got to be that diva bitch. 'Cause if not, you'll end up being that dumb bitch that wished she would have been. You choose."

"But, Raylon said—"

"Fuck what Raylon said, Shoney. You know for a fact the nigga cheating, and that alone should be more than enough."

Quiet as kept, Sept was right, but I was yet to become the bitch I needed to be when it came to being married to a man like Raylon. But like she said, I had to choose, and I was hoping like hell I'd choose wisely.

***

Raylon

Once I received the text confirming who was all in attendance at the Shack, I hurried home to give Shoney her surprise, because there was no way I was about to miss out on all the money that was sure to be won and lost. Several guys were there from the OKC, and word was they were looking for high-stake bets for when the horses ran. I'd been thinking of venturing into the races for a while, and to hear about it from the guys that were already into it, I felt now was the time for me to do so.

I pulled into the lot of the Shack and immediately spotted the automobiles of a few players I hadn't seen before. The sleek, heavy-duty trucks and several Bentley Continentals were parked near the rear of the building, which also let me know they were newcomers. It was always understood amongst regulars that the front belonged to those of us who had tabs and were known for paying them. After parking in my usual spot and grabbing $8,000 from the stash compartment of my truck, I made my way inside.

"Wassup, Raylon!" someone yelled from the section over.

When seeing a group of guys I didn't know, I turned to see who called me, then I held up my hand and waved towards the voice. My first order of business was checking in with those in attendance, and handing over the money I was carrying.

"Raylon, nigga, where you been? I've been telling these country ass niggas you'd have been here by now," said Wayne.

Wayne was one of the guys that co-owned the Shack and took pride in how much money walked through his place of business. He also made sure the heavy betters all knew each other. Because when it was all said and done, we'd be the ones either owing or paying, and when it came to either, Wayne made sure things went well. I nodded, grabbed my ticket from the horse man, then turned and told him, "Had to take care of something at the house. What's up?"

"Hell, I'm trying to keep the money flowing. These horse-riding ass niggas got money, Raylon, and they ain't got half the game needed to keep it."

I looked from Wayne to where a couple of guys and a few women sat in a booth not too far from where we stood. I didn't recognize either of them. "Them hoes came with them too?" I asked, knowing how the game was played when niggas called themselves baiting the lines.

"Yeah. The thing is, the hoes pulled up in the Bentleys, and they the ones been dropping the cash."

I smiled at the light-complected chick wearing the pinstriped pantsuit, nodded at the guys, and turned back to Wayne. "What they talking about?"

"They waiting on you. You already know you one of our heavy hitters. Ever since Four Fingers and them dun' went and got themselves killed, it's only a few of y'all left."

His words brought a smile to my face, because there were a few of us left, and it just so happened that they were either on my team, or wanted to be. I told him, "Let's crank this shit up, then see if I can get the keys to one of them Continentals out there."

One thing I knew for sure was that when you got deep enough in a motherfucker's pockets, you got into their heads, and by the way the hoes they came with were looking, it was all about the head games. And by the way they pulled up, their pockets were deep as hell. Before all was said and done, I just might have to call my boys. There was always that possibility.

***

Brent

Despite the text I'd sent to both Raylon and Daxx, I was the only one that showed to oversee the renovations of the detail shop. The building itself needed a few repairs, but what I wanted to provide was a one-stop shop for our customers. Them having to go elsewhere for anything was something I didn't want, and that was something I wanted to address with my boys, but it was as if they had other things to do. With the additional stalls, I wanted new car lifts added, a new part for oil and transmission services, and a wheel and tire service center.

I'd already ordered a shipment of rims and tires, bought all kinds of touchscreen head units, keyless starters, screens, rearview monitors, and all sorts of accessories for automobiles. Matter of fact, the guys had not too long ago finished servicing Shoney's M5, and several other luxury cars. Being that detailing cars and trucks wasn't my thing, I went and hired a couple of guys that recently graduated from one of the auto body and repair schools, as well as a couple of technicians. Thanks to Sheila, we were now providing people with legit jobs and minimum wage income.

I was exiting my office when a Range Rover pulled in front of the building, and a familiar face climbed out. I smiled when seeing Sheila because quiet as kept, I liked the way she rolled.

"Looks like business is booming."

I gave Sheila a side hug, a quick smooch on the cheek, and released her. Things were cordial and professional with us, and I didn't want her to think anything other than that. "Thanks to you," I told her before opening the door and allowing her entry.

"Now all you need to do is get rid of that car you got."

For the longest, she'd been trying to get me to buy another ride, but I wasn't tripping. Besides, I was too busy putting money elsewhere.

"I will." In due time.

I, first, had to make sure things were as they should be with both the car lot and the shop. I walked Sheila around the shop, so she could see where the money was going, and once I told her about some of the additions and upgrades I wanted, she only nodded. It was evident that she had a few things on her mind because she wasn't her usual self. To show both my concern, and the fact that I was able to recognize it, I asked her, "Are you alright?"

"Yeah, yeah, I'm good. Why you ask?"

For a brief second, I caught myself feeling lost in her hazel-green eyes. Her caramel complexion seemed to glow under the lighting above. "Um, you seem reserved today, is all."

"Am I that transparent?"

I smiled seeing Sheila smile. My shoulders rose and fell. I nodded. "Normally, you're hyped about something, but today, you seem a little down. Like you could use an ear."

"Matter of fact, I could use an ear, Brent, but would you know anything about divorce and marriage?"

Sheila gave me one of those tilted head expressions, as if she knew I knew nothing of the sort. And instead of dismissing the idea of traveling down one of the many roads in her mind, I told her, "Try me."

I took a seat next to the one she sat in, instead of sitting behind my desk, because I wanted to show her that we were equal. There was no little her and big me. We were partners. Business partners.

"Well, Brian's dad has him for the next week, and my mind was there, I guess."

I watched Sheila sigh after disclosing that information. She'd already told me what kind of man her son's dad was, reasons why they weren't together now, but I also understood where the child's father was coming from wanting to continue seeing his kid.

I told her, "You know what, Sheila? Their relationship is going to be one you have no control over. I know you feel as if you have to be up on everything, but you're going to have to let him be what he is to him. You already said he was a good dad, and a great provider for his son, so let that outweigh the fact that you all's relationship—or marriage—didn't work out. That's a man that's trying to do right by his son, and you really don't want to be the one to stand in the way of that."

"I guess you're my mind reader now, huh?"

"I'm an expression reader. I knew something wasn't right when you pulled up and Brian wasn't in tow."

"Yeah, well, I just don't want there to come a time where he feels Brian's well-being is with him and where he is."

I shook my head with closed eyes. "He knows what type of woman you are, Sheila. You're strong minded, strong willed, and the perfect mother, and he knows where you stand. And I seriously doubt if he wants to see you in court again." I smiled with those last words, 'cause she'd already hit the man harder than most.

"Well, thanks for the compliments, Brent, but right now, I'm not feeling so strong. My son is my weakness, and he knows that."

Sheila and I talked until one of the technicians knocked on my office door, asking for her keys. I always made sure her rides were detailed and cleaned when she did arrive, but being that today was not scheduled, I wasn't expecting her.

"Come on. Let's take a walk. I want to show you something." I walked Sheila to the corner of the lot and pointed across the street at the building sitting adjacent to the Wing Stop restaurant. "I want that building next. Once I get things stationed over here and flip a few dollars, I want the building."

"For what? You already have—"

I cut her off with a shake of my head. I knew she was thinking I wanted to expand the detail shop, but actually, I wanted to turn it into a beauty supply shop. September had said something about it being needed in this area, and I was wanting to surprise her with that. "A beauty supply shop. That's what I want to put right there."

"A beauty supply? Whose idea was that?"

I half-shrugged, half-smiled, and looked over at her. "September's."

"September gets the world from you, Brent. Speaking of her, how'd she like the car?"

Sheila knew that it was because of her I was able to afford something I normally wouldn't have, but she didn't rub it in my face like Daxx or Raylon. She liked the fact that I was a keeper when it came to Sept. But like all people, she threw in her two cents when it came to the way I should have been treated in return.

"She loves it. Drives it damn near every day," I told her. And since she was throwing Sept in the air of our conversation, I decided to do the same to her. "So, how are things with you and Daxx?"

Sheila didn't smile, and at first, acted as if she didn't hear the question. Then she shrugged and said, "Daxx isn't relationship material. There's no fifty-fifty when it comes to him. He expects women to play by his rules, and that's not the direction I'm trying to go. Been there, and couldn't do it."

I knew exactly what she was talking about, but when Daxx was the one giving the visual of the way things were with him and Sheila, he made sure it was believed that things were perfect, and she'd said as much on several occasions.

I told her, "Give him time. He'll figure it out."

"And me having figured things out for myself and my son doesn't matter?"

"No, no. I'm not saying that at all, Sheila. You know me better than that. All I'm saying is…"

If I did have the words to say, I couldn't find them because I fell silent, and her expression soured. What could be said to a woman that had her mind made up? She'd dealt with men many times before—wrote some off and kept it moving. One thing I liked about Sheila was that she knew what she wanted, and she didn't play any games when it came to getting it.

"Oh, now the cat got your tongue?"

Whether it was an inside joke, or just something innocently said, we both smiled at the statement. 'Cause this was the first time she'd made it, or was this the first time I had no comeback?

"Let's go see what they're doing to your truck."

"Yeah, that's what I thought, Big Boy."

Sheila punched me on the side of my stomach as we headed back towards the building. She'd finally gotten comfortable around me enough to where the vibe between us was damn near like the one I shared with my girl, Sept. If I wasn't with September, I could definitely see myself with Sheila.

***

Shoney

After making a few stops, September and I found ourselves walking in and out of the many boutiques in the Galleria. She and I both bought whatever we liked and things we really didn't have to, but I wasn't about to let her go overboard. And that began the conversation she brought up about the $16,000 Christopher Kane bags I pulled her away from.

"Oh, don't worry. I'll have that bitch before the month's out," she promised.

"I don't give a damn how much money I have. I am not going to spend that much on a bag, Sept. Are you crazy?"

"Just imagine what them broke ass bitches at work will be saying when I walk in with that bitch on my shoulder."

I laughed, grabbed my girl by the arm, and told her, "Probably the same shit they been saying since day one."

"And Alyssa? I started to beat the bitch's ass the other day, Shoney. That hoe really thinks because she's bigger than me that I won't smear shit on her ass."

I covered my girl's mouth when seeing some of the people we'd passed look at her as if she was crazy. Despite me knowing for sure that she was serious, there was still an image I needed for her to display when we were in public.

"Hey, excuse me, ladies, but I couldn't help but notice that you two are the most beautiful women here, and I just had to steal a moment of you all's time," said a tall, dark-complected brother wearing creased slacks and a nice white dress shirt with gold cufflinks.

The smile I wore widened more than it should have, and my eyes did stay trained on him a little too long, but I bounced back when holding out my left hand, displaying the huge diamond ring Raylon bought me a few months ago. September, on the other hand, got the hook and bait he threw, and twirled it around her finger. I only rolled my eyes.

"I don't know about her, but my pussy pays bills."

"Sept!" I screamed, knowing I should have pulled her along instead of entertaining the guy in the first place. Once again, I looked around to see who might be seeing us.

"What kind of bills you talking?" he asked, moving closer to Sept and away from me.

"Please don't pay her any mind. She's had a little too many coolers," I lied. The last thing I needed was for him to know that she was this way sober.

"Um, I just put down on my house, and the mortgage is $2000 alone. Then, there's my car note, and I like to go shopping."

I pulled Sept away from the guy and gave him a quick wave. "Sept, will you stop that? Nigga already thinks you're serious."

"Hell, I am serious. My pussy ain't free, and my time damn sure ain't."

To say my girl didn't have a filter was an understatement, but there should have been a place and time for everything. However, when it came to Sept, neither existed.

"Ouuu, bitch, I like that outfit, and that suit," I told her while pointing to the items being displayed in a men's store.

"Shoney, we ain't here to spend shit on Raylon, or any other nigga for that matter."

"I just said I liked it, Sept. It would look good on him, though." One thing about Raylon, was that the nigga could dress and didn't mind spending on the things he liked. That went for us as well. While looking at some of the clothes being displayed, a thought came to mind. It had been a while since I'd bought Raylon anything, and a nice surprise would definitely have its reward. I was sure. "Let's see what else they got, Sept. You might even see something for Brent in here." I pulled her towards the entrance of the store, saw a couple of workers, and pointed to the suit I saw. "Do you guys tailor them also?"

"See, that's your problem now, Shoney. Everything is always about Raylon, Raylon, Raylon. Girl, fuck that nigga."

"Sept, he is my husband, and this is what married people do. We give and receive." I walked over to where more of the selection was and pointed. "I'd love to see him in that one," I told her—talking about the green and grey silk shirt that cost $300.

"Give and receive, huh? So, we are talking about giving and receiving now?"

I rolled my eyes because I already knew where she was heading. It wasn't that long ago that we found out that Raylon was giving to more than just me when it came to things he liked. Now that he owned a few credit cards, bills came to the house, and it was Sept that actually went into a letter addressed to him and found out he'd either taken some bitch shopping, or allowed her to use a credit card. That was something I was sure he wouldn't do again, and as a matter of fact, it was something I made him promise not to.

"Can I please go a day without being reminded of something Raylon's done in the past?"

"I wish I was your man. I'd have your ass walking around drenched in mud every day."

"Whatever, tramp. If you were my man, you'd be breaking yourself the same way Raylon is now."

"Bitch, that nigga spending crumbs on you."

"And let you tell it, I'm spending crumbs on him. His crumbs, matter of fact."

After selecting two pairs of the slacks I liked, a couple of dress shirts, and a set of cufflinks to match, I paid cash for the $850 purchase.

"A pair of socks, some clean boxers for his nasty ass, and some rubbers. That's what you need to be buying him."

"Next time, Sept. If that makes you smile, I'll buy exactly that the next time."

Back at the car, Sept snatched my key fob from me and told me to let her drive. She'd been comparing her Lexus to my convertible since before we got them, and now that we did, I couldn't keep her from behind the wheel. I was just about to check my appearance in the mirror when we both heard a low humming sound.

"What did you just do, Sept?" I asked.

"The hell if I know. All I did was put my seatbelt on."

I retraced my actions and turned the rearview mirror back to where it was previously set. The humming started again.

"What the—"

It wasn't until the second time I turned the rearview mirror all the way towards the right did we hear the humming sound again, but this time, we also noticed the dash above the touchscreen had raised slightly. Sept was the one that opened it fully.

"Ouuu, bitch. Jackpot!"

There was a compartment hidden there, and the contents in it were sure to have been left behind by someone. And from the looks of it, it wouldn't be long before they came for it.

"Put it back, Sept. We don't know who that belongs to." Those words fell on deaf ears, because not only was Sept pulling the stacks of cash from the stash spot, but she was counting them.

"I know exactly whose it is. Your black ass just don't realize it yet."

There was no way Raylon would be that careless, and there was no way he'd just stash such a huge amount of cash in my car. He wasn't allowed to do that anymore.

"He knows I don't play this shit, Sept."

"This might not even have shit to do with Raylon. Brent did say the car was confiscated in another state. The owner might have been a hustling motherfucker, Shoney. This is about $60,000 cash, and if I were you, I'd pocket this shit and don't say shit about it."

"And when someone comes looking for they money?" I asked, and the moment I did, I knew it was the dumbest thing to do.

Sept only fanned herself with a stack of bills and began stuffing the rest in her purse. "Then you just tell them I got it, because we ain't giving shit back."

"And what if Raylon just so happened to put it there thinking I wouldn't stumble across it?"

Once again, the expression she wore told me what she thought of that idea. "You tell the nigga the cops pulled us over and took it. I'll bet you he ain't going to run up in the police station talking about no missing money. Problem solved."

I sighed, applied another coat of the amber-colored lip gloss I wore, and fastened my seatbelt. Tonight, while Raylon and I were in bed, I'd subtly bring up the money, and if it just so happened he didn't know about it, I'd leave it at that. But if he did call himself using my car for a stash spot, I was going to give him a piece of my mind, and if I had to, I was going to kick his ass.

***

Daxx

Something had been telling me to get back at Brent when he texted me, and knowing how he was when it came to making a move, that should have been the first thing I did. But money was coming up short at one of the spots, and I was really thinking of a way to handle it without involving the guys. I, instead, made the trip to the shop to see what he had going on and was glad I did when seeing Sheila's Range Rover being serviced. She'd been dodging a nigga for a while, and it was about time I'd put my foot on her neck. The bitch was a moneymaker, and I had to keep her in my corner. I parked, climbed out, and made my way inside.

"What's up, Daxx?"

I threw the deuce to a couple of guys and continued on. I had my mind on one thing: Sheila.

"Why haven't you called me back?" I asked her, intentionally interrupting the conversation they were having. Sometimes, a bitch had to know when a nigga meant business.

"Hello to you too, Daxx. But I do believe we were having a conversation of our own," Brent stated.

"I've been busy, I guess," she told me.

I walked closer to where she sat and said, "You around here playing these games like a nigga going to sweat you, and that's not what I'm about, Sheila. I'm really with the shits." The second she chose to look elsewhere, I grabbed her chin and turned her to face me. Sheila was a beautiful woman, but what she needed was a stomp-down nigga to humble her.

"Will you please let me go, Daxx?"

I stepped back as she stood. Being that she was so much shorter than me, my towering figure dwarfed her. There was power there, and I knew she was feeling my presence. "Is that what you really want?"

For the past couple of months, Sheila and I had been going back and forth in our so-called "friendship" or "relationship." We'd gone out a few times, and really nothing more, but I needed for her to know it was going to be my way or no way. She knew she wanted me and knew what I was about when it came to making money, and that's what mattered most. I watched her sigh in defeat. Her shoulders rose and fell.

"I have a lot on my mind, Daxx," she said while grabbing her purse.

I might have been hard on a bitch, but I was also understanding, and that was the reason why I grabbed her hand and said, "I really do care for you, Sheila, and you know that. How about I take you out tonight? Help you relax a bit. You already know everything's on me."

"I, um…"

"Come on, Sheila. I got you." I gently massaged her hand, knowing she'd break. The last time we went out, I knew I could have fucked her, but I had other things to do, and laying up all night wasn't one of them. But tonight, I had to get the edge off somehow, and Sheila seemed to be the perfect outlet.

"Okay, cool, but none of the last time mess, Daxx. I don't care about where your people hang, or the ways in which you make your money."

"I got you. I got you. Chill. I'll get at you around eight o'clock," I told her, knowing exactly what she needed.

Brent and I watched her climb into her truck and pull off. She blew her horn and waved. We both acknowledged her in our own way, and once she was out of view, Brent turned to me and asked a bevy of stupid ass questions.

"Nigga, are you high?"

I turned back towards the entrance of the shop, checked my watch, and smiled. I told him, "I'm going to fuck the shit out of that bitch tonight."

"You fucking with that shit again, Daxx?"

"Nigga, I got this," I told him, knowing how he got when he thought I was high.

"Don't fuck off what we got going on, Daxx. You back on that shit again, and you know what happened the last time. Does Raylon know about—"

"Will you chill the fuck out! I'm the one keeping this shit together for all of us. I'm the one making sure the money keeps coming from these streets." I faced Brent, looked him square in his eyes, and said, "I got this, homie. I know what's at stake, but it's about time one of us locked the bitch in, anyway. All that bitch needs is some dick, nigga. You'll see."

Brent was too busy licking this hoe's wounds when he should have been licking her ass, but the nigga was on some other shit, steady worried about September's messy ass. As of now, we paid Sheila for damn near everything she did for us, but before all was said and done with, I was going to have the bitch working for free.

Chapter Three

Raylon

The $16,000 I lost at the Shack was partly because I had to do a little baiting of my own, and we needed to keep these guys coming back. Not only could I have broken the bank with their asses, I could have snatched the darker woman because she continually stayed under me. And we both knew it had nothing to do with who she came with, or the reasons they were here.

"Are you sure you don't want any action at that money, Raylon?" the short, chubby guy asked while looking over the ticket I'd given him.

"Maybe next time. That's pocket change, and I've really enjoyed you all's company." I made sure I was looking directly into the eyes of the thick, dark-complected chick while saying that. I had to see her again.

"The next time you're in the OKC, we're going to show you a real good time, Raylon. You can bet on that," said the taller of the trio.

I ordered another round of drinks for the guys, and another bottle of Cîroc for the ladies. It was now time to go to the real money. "So, what's the buy-in on the next race?" I asked before pulling the chocolate stallion onto my lap. She needed to know what my intentions were, and the fact that I didn't mind paying to play.

"Fifty grand. If your horse is in the top three, you triple your money, and if the motherfucker pulls in first, you got yourself a half a million dollars," he replied in his southern accent.

"And everything is straight across the board?" With that much money in play, it was best to get that understood off the top.

"I'll put the money up for you, and you just give me my shit back," said the woman sitting on my lap.

I smiled, clasped her right thigh, and told her, "I don't even know your name, but you're willing to put up that much money? It's got to be more to it."

"Let's just say, it'll be our pot if you win. By the way, I'm Cindy."

If there was a lie to be told, that was sure to be it. But, hey? We weren't here to become friends, and the only names needing to be known were the ones we were betting on. I told him, "Summer's Gold. That's who I'm riding with."

As soon as numbers were exchanged, promises were made, and they were on their way. Cindy pulled me to the side, started her maroon-colored Bentley with a key fob, and told me, "I could use a nigga like you from time to time." She then looked down at the bulge in my slacks and licked her lips seductively.

"Likewise," I told her while looking around to see who might be seeing our interaction. When feeling the vibration of my phone, I pulled it out and handed it to her. "Fill me in so we can make this personal."

"It was personal the moment I saw you, Raylon, so let the other bitch know we playing for keeps," Cindy said before climbing into her car and handing me back my phone.

To confirm the information she gave me, I pressed send, and as soon as her phone began to glow, I shook my head and told her, "Ain't no other bitches to play with."

"Well, your wedding ring says different."

With that, she pulled off and was gone, and as soon as I was in the cabin of my own truck, I called Daxx. We had to put something together, because I had to be in that buy-in.

***

Shoney

Raylon promised that he'd be home earlier tonight, and against my best judgement and past experiences, I held him to it. I'd gotten me a nice workout on my elliptical machine and even squeezed in a quick abs routine before cleaning, starting dinner, and a hot shower. All of me wished that Raylon would walk in while I bathed myself and make me feel like the woman I was. But there was still a part of me that accepted the reality that despite the promise he made about coming home, that might not even happen. But like always, I was that bitch that stayed on the phone and peeked out of the window every now and again, hoping to see the headlights of his truck pulling up.

Even then, I still played as if I was either sleeping or busy, and at the same time, excited to see him. I looked over the dinner I was preparing, closed my eyes, and shook my head because he should have been here by now, and when I did call his cell, it went straight to voicemail. There was no telling which bitch he was with tonight, and that made me feel some type of way. They knew he was married and should have at least sent him home, but these were the types of hoes he fucked off on me for.

Once dinner was ready, he still hadn't shown or called, and I was deeper in my feelings. I prayed nothing happened to him to where he couldn't call at least, but the past reminded me of how foolish I was even thinking that was the reason. Instead of sweating his phone and filling it with the *I miss you* texts and the *love you* emoji, I fixed my plate, ate, and left his in the microwave. I laughed at the thought of me pouring all the rest of the food in the trashcan and leaving the lid open for him to see, but I had put my all into preparing this meal, and if he just so happened to bring his ass home in the next few minutes, or an hour even, he'd know that.

Just as I was about to clean a few dishes, my phone startled me. I then hurried to see who the caller was, and to my surprise, it was my husband. I answered as if all was cool. "Hey, babe. What's up? Where you at?" That was a question I didn't want to ask but somehow did.

"Babe, this shit is crazy over here. The cops just took one of our runners to jail, so now I'm having to go bond his dumb ass out. Luckily, he didn't get caught with anything."

"Be careful out there, Raylon. You know I don't like you dealing with them people." I immediately thought about my husband paying for the mistakes of another and everything falling back on me and what we'd built for ourselves. There were always those thoughts.

"I'm handling it, babe. What you got goin' on?"

"Well, I cooked, sorted some things out, and can't wait until you come home," I told him, hoping it would bring him to me.

"Let me finish up over here, and I'll be home shortly, babe. I love you."

Those three words alone let me know that he wasn't in the presence of some other bitch, and if he was, she now knew she didn't mean shit to him. I hoped. And knowing he would give the chore to someone else, I asked him, "Where's Daxx and Brent?"

"Daxx is here with me, and Brent had to make a run. He should be back shortly himself."

"Oh, alright then. See you soon, babe." After ending the call with Raylon, I phoned Sept. It was always something when it came to the shit Raylon and the rest of the guys were dealing with.

"What is it now, Shoney?"

"Hello to you too, September." I walked from my dining area, up the stairs to my bedroom, pulled off the t-shirt I was wearing, and stepped out of my tights. There would be no sexy greetings tonight. I was sure. "Guess what happened now?" I knew those words would provide me with answers, and if not, they'd pique her curiosity.

"What he do now, Shoney?"

I crawled to the head of my bed and sat with my back against the headboard. This was the position I found myself in until I heard my husband enter the security code downstairs. "One of their workers got jammed up, and they're on their way to make his bond. That's why he ain't home—"

"Is that what that nigga told you?"

"Yeah, I just got off the phone with him just now," I told her before crossing my legs at the ankles and reaching for my remote.

"Well, I just got off the phone with Brent, and he ain't said shit about no runner, or paying anybody's bond."

"Well, that's what Raylon said. What are you—" Before I could ask, I heard Brent's voice on the other end. She'd merged the call so I could hear it from the horse's mouth.

"Hey, Sept, what's up?"

"I thought you said you were on your way, Brent? I don't have time for no games, nigga. My pussy itching, and I'm cramping."

"I'm a couple of blocks from your spot, as we speak. What you trippin' on?"

"I thought you were with Daxx and Raylon, 'cause Shoney just hung up, and she said—"

"Sept, you know that nigga be lying his ass off. The last I heard, the nigga was at the Shack, and Daxx is out with Sheila."

Even though I'd been through this a hundred times, it seemed like I still felt my heart break whenever it happened. I did everything a good woman could do, and somehow, still got treated as if I was the worst bitch a nigga could have. The thing that continued to get to me was that he didn't even have to lie about the shit he was doing. All I asked was that he respected me enough to put me first.

"So, you don't know shit about him having to bond some guy out of jail?" Sept got answers out of Brent without even asking, and the more she drilled him, the more trouble he thought he was in.

"I'm telling you, Sept, if he does, I have not been informed yet."

"Well, hurry up and get here before I change my mind about giving you this pussy."

"I'll be there within seconds."

Sept ended the call with him and said, "So, don't tell me shit about what ya lying ass husband said, Shoney. That's why I bleed his ass."

"I'm sick of this shit, Sept. I cook, clean, I keep myself right for this nigga, and he still—"

Sept cut me off with a closing statement of her own. "Keep his foot in your ass."

"He's not with no bitch because he did say he loved me, and he wasn't whispering," I told her.

"And what the hell is that supposed to mean, Shoney? Do you know how many times I've been with a nigga and they say some shit like that to their girlfriends and wives? Bitches know they position, Shoney."

"Well, it didn't sound like he was with no bitch. He might have been at that damn gambling shack, but he wasn't with no bitch." I scrolled through my contacts until I found Raylon's number. All I had to do was touch the screen and call, but I wasn't going to be one of those bitches. For now, I would also play my position.

"Can I go now, Shoney? Brent is pulling up right now."

"Nasty ass, tramp." I laughed before ending the call.

At least she had someone to get nasty with. I'd been thinking about what I wanted to do to Raylon all day, but none of it was yet to happen, and when he did show, if he showed, the last thing he was going to get was some hot pussy. I promise you that.

***

Daxx

I did appreciate the fact that Raylon was including me in a nice lick, but that should have been something he could have easily done himself, and that was the reason I asked him, "So, you've been fucking off all that money, Raylon?"

"Nigga, I got the money. I just did a count, and right now, I can't buy in until we flip this next drop. And I need the money by tomorrow."

"How much are we talking?" I smiled when seeing Sheila's Range Rover pull into the parking lot of the restaurant we agreed to meet at. I'd been waiting on her for the past twenty minutes and was just about to write her off.

"Fifty grand."

"I'm going to stop by the house tomorrow. I want my shit back, nigga. I'm not tripping on the horse—that's if you win. But I do need my—"

"Nigga, you acting like I'm some walk-up or something. Fifty grand ain't shit. Hell, all I gotta do is place within the top three, and I'll give you that back, and some."

"Yeah, yeah. I got you. I've got to go."

I hung up before Raylon could drag with one of his "he's got it all under control" speeches. That nigga had that bad, and if you were to listen to him, you'd be all the way under the game he was serving.

I pushed my phone into my pocket and smiled. Sheila was definitely a dime, and in more ways than one, she reminded me of September. "I was starting to think you weren't going to make it," I told her the minute she walked toward me. The full-length, wrap-around dress she wore had me thinking of what was and wasn't under it, and that was something I was dying to find out before we parted ways.

"Let's just say my tardiness wasn't planned."

I tipped the valet, placed my hand on the small of Sheila's back, and led her into the establishment. Once we were seated at the small but nice table for two, I pulled out a Chapstick tube and asked, "You want to take the edge off?" I pushed the cocaine-filled tube towards her.

"And what is this, Daxx?"

I laughed, pinched my nose, and leaned forward. I whispered, "Some of the best shit in the world. That's called 'winter white' right there."

"You're offering me drugs, Daxx? Are you serious right now?"

The expression Sheila wore seemed to bring out her features more. The more she squinted her eyes and scrunched her face, the more she reminded me of Sept. It was always the hoes who acted as if they'd never tooted the powder before who turned out to be straight-up addicts. And with Sheila having the perfect good-girl image, there had to be something floating the boat she paddled.

"You just seemed a little stiff, and—"

"Well, drugs definitely are not going to loosen me up any. I can't believe you brought drugs in the restaurant, Daxx. You really have lost your mind."

"I'm just looking out for you." I reached for the small tube and placed it back inside of my pocket, knowing she'd ask about it before the night was over.

***

Brent

As soon as Sept opened the door, I handed her the envelope containing the $3,000 she needed, along with the three-ounce bottle of Miss Dior perfume I thought she'd like. I told her, "That's a new eau de toilette." I watched her examine the small box and smile.

"You're making sure you get the pussy tonight."

I walked past her while saying, "Sept, you trippin'. I always bring you something when I come."

"Oh, really?"

I heard the words I spoke after they were said and knew right off she thought I was being funny. I corrected myself. "You know what I'm talkin' 'bout, babe."

"Bring your big ass on here before I hand you this shit back."

I followed Sept into the living room area, never once taking my eyes off her petite ass. The panties she wore wedged between her butt, and the right side was slightly higher than the left. The little t-shirt she was wearing was apparently used to cover something else, because it did nothing to hide what I was seeing. I took a seat next to her, then watched her fold her legs under and thumb through the bills I'd given her. I always broke bread with Sept and always would.

"Looks like you had a pretty good week."

"Yeah, you can say that. I got half of that from Daxx. Raylon still hasn't given me my cut, so when he does, I'm going to throw you some more." I reached over, grabbed her legs, and pulled them onto my lap. I loved massaging September's feet. She happily obliged.

"The nigga fucks off more money than he makes. I'm surprised he ain't been asking you for any."

"Them niggas make damn near eight grand a month fucking with that shit. He better not pull up on me asking for no money." I raised her leg, stole a peek at the pussy, and kissed her toes. "Ummm."

"Why that nigga ain't putting that shit in the bank? That don't make no damn sense for him to be stashing all that money at Shoney's house."

"Yeah. I be telling him the same thing. He be thinking Sheila too far in his business, so he keep the numbers away from her."

"Speaking of Sheila, you sure she ain't doing no funny shit?"

I shook my head, dismissing that idea totally. It was always that Sheila walked me through statements, transactions, and every other thing that had to do with our finances. "Hell naw. I make sure she gets paid her percentage. She even makes sure the funds are deposited into my account first. She hasn't shown me anything but professionality so far."

"Let me find out you fucking that bitch, Brent."

"Girl, ain't nobody fucking Sheila. Business is business between us." I thought about those words and added. "At least with me and Raylon. Daxx, on the other hand, he's another story."

"Watch that nigga, Brent, because he'll fuck up a wet dream for a bitch. He'll be the motherfucker making a bitch wake up from inside the dream."

We laughed. I went from massaging her feet to her thighs. I told her, "He'd better not fuck it up. He already owes her, like, $4,000, and I'm going to make sure she gets that. Even if I have to pay for it myself."

"Knowing his sad ass, that's exactly what he wants you to do."

I nodded. "That's why I did what you told me to do a long time ago. I keep the keys to the vaults."

"*We* keep the keys to the vaults, nigga." With that being said, Sept raised her hips so I could pull off her panties. I swallowed hard when she opened her legs and began rubbing her clit. "You know what time it is, Big Boy."

I raised up, then positioned myself so that she'd hang slightly off the edge of the couch, and raised both her legs to where her calves rested on my shoulders. I loved when she held me by both sides of my face and fed me the pussy. I loved when she did that shit.

"Eat my shit, nigga. Do me right."

Sept was one of the cleanest women I knew, and that was the reason I pushed her legs back further and stuck half of my tongue in her ass, plus, two fingers in her pussy, and pressed my thumb against her clit at the same time. I knew what my girl liked.

"Ouuu, shit, nigga, spend your money, baby. Spend your motherfucking money..."

***

Shoney

When the security system did finally beep, alerting me that someone had entered my home, it was 4:40 AM. I'd waited up half the night for Raylon's lying ass and knew exactly what I was going to say once he did come home. But now that he was here, I only turned towards my side of the room. My back would be to him whenever he did enter. I could feel my heart beating in my chest—could hear the continual ringing noise in my ears, so I knew I was mad as hell. This nigga had me fucked up, for real.

The moment I heard him enter our room, I inhaled as deeply as I could. If he did wear the scent of some bitch, that would be the first thing to hit me, but to my surprise, the Saint Laurent cologne I'd bought him permeated the air. I sighed my relief, but when noticing him head towards the shower, instead of kissing my cheek like he did whenever he found me asleep, the familiar warm feeling swept over me. His actions told me that he hadn't showered at some bitch's house—which I was grateful for—and that he was trying to rid himself of some filth. Some stinky-mouth bitch must have sucked his dick before sending him home. Instead of rolling over and acknowledging his presence, I continued to play dead.

"Shoney, you awake?"

Not only did he whisper the shit, but he had to ask some shit like that. I remained still but opened my eyes.

"Babe?"

Me not being able to see him, touch him, and wrap my arms around him was the reason I broke. I pretended to have just been awakened. "Raylon? What time is it?" I yawned, stretched a bit, and rolled over to where I could see him. "You just getting home, babe?" I watched my husband undress, hang his slacks and shirt, and step out of his boxers/briefs. I started to tell him to toss them to me so I could smell them but decided to wait until he'd stepped into the shower. I, instead, asked. "Did you eat your plate?"

"I'm about to tackle it as soon as I get out of this shower, baby. Thanks."

If I had something to throw at his ass, I would have been thrown it, but I had to say this. When the nigga thanked me for shit, I found myself less mad.

"You want me to join you?" That's the way I learned that it was something he didn't want me to know about or see when he told me no and that he'd only be a minute. It surprised the hell out of me when he said yes. I watched his dick from where I laid—felt myself swallow the lump forming in my throat and slowly climbed out of bed. I'd already told myself that if I did smell some bitch on him or saw some hickeys or scratches that I wasn't going to give him shit, and I meant it. "You know how I feel about you dealing with them people, Raylon."

I knew the nigga was lying his ass off about having to go downtown, but I still welcomed his conversation. It also gave me time and a way to examine him.

"That motherfucker cost me $20,000, and half of my day."

I stepped into the shower behind Raylon, checked his back, the back of his neck, and his ass, because those were the main places I marked up when he fucked me down. Seeing nothing new, I grabbed the towel from him and began lathering him with suds. He turned to face me and pulled my locs, so I'd be forced to look up at him, and began sucking my lips and kissing my neck. "Will you stop so I can bathe you, Raylon?" His dick hardened under my touch.

"I want some of this chocolate ass you got, babe."

"Raylon, it's late, and I do have to get up early. If only you'd come home earlier." I fought him with what I could while letting him know that I was expecting him at a decent hour.

"Come on, Shoney. Please, babe?"

Before I could put up more of a fight, Raylon scooped me up, slid the shower door open with his foot, and carried me to the bathroom counter. He placed himself between my legs.

"Raylon, I…" He began sucking on my ear and massaging my titties, making me balance myself with both hands, as I couldn't push him away. I loved when Raylon took the pussy. "Babe..."

"Open your legs wider, Shoney. Give me some of this pussy, babe."

When feeling Raylon bite down on my neck, I complied with his demands and wrapped my legs as high up on his back as I could. His aggressiveness alone proved to me that he hadn't had any pussy. I sucked air through my teeth when he entered, raised slightly to stroke his ego, and told him how good he felt. "Hurry up, 'cause I need to get some sleep, Raylon."

For twenty-two minutes straight, Raylon sexed me in two positions. If I wasn't hefted up on the counter, I was bent over it, and when he felt himself about to nut, he pulled out, made me change position again, and tongued the pussy. I didn't know what had gotten into him, but I was glad it did.

After another shower myself, I snuggled up under Raylon while he laid on his back. I stroked his middle and made small circles around his chest. It was times like these that melted my hardened exterior and just brought the softness out of me. "I'm going in late today, babe."

"You don't even have to go at all, Shoney. I don't know why you put up with that shit in the first place."

Raylon was right, and for the umpteenth time, I debated whether or not to call and say I'm never coming back. I had money now, and truth be told, I was sitting on enough to rent me a nice space and start me a fitness class. That was one of the things I really wanted to do, and let September tell it, we'd do that and more when the time was right.

I glanced at the clock. It was right at 6 AM, and I closed my eyes. I'd get me an hour of sleep before going to work. Hell, as many times as I'd helped Mr. Dillan out, he shouldn't even trip. Me questioning Raylon about the money Sept and I found would be done at another time, because the pussy put him straight to sleep. It always did.

Chapter Four

Shoney

By the time I finally awoke, Raylon was nowhere to be found, and the clock on my nightstand told me it was about to be 9 AM.

"Shit!"

I hurried to get myself together. I had a ton of things to do today and should have been checking them off by now. It angered me that Raylon didn't think of me enough to wake me, but when thinking about it, he didn't want me going to work, anyway. After making my way through the house and into the kitchen, I noticed that he'd eaten and put away his dish, which let me know that either he'd just walked through the door, or that he'd been up. I knew my man.

With me being in such a hurry, I threw on a pair of form-fitting jeans, a loose blouse I could tie in the front, and stepped into a pair of lace-up booties. I let my locks hang under the silk scarf wrapped around it, applied some lip gloss to my lips, and was done. I was just about to head to my garage when the doorbell rang twice.

"Who the fuck?" Instead of grabbing the key fob to my M6, I grabbed the keys to my Tacoma and went to see who was making me later than I already was. I swung the door open. "Daxx?"

"Hey, Shoney. Where that nigga at?"

I shrugged and told him, "The hell if I know. He was gone when I got up." I grabbed the small bag he held and closed my front door behind me. *I'll walk around to the garage,* I thought.

Instead of Daxx stepping back so I would walk past him, he only stood there. He smiled and told me, "You a pretty, black motherfucker, Shoney."

"Are you alright, Daxx?" I grew annoyed, urged him backward, and began walking down the stairs.

"And that ass looking real nice, Shoney."

Daxx followed me all the way around to the garage while giving me compliments for my ass, and the things I was wearing. He continually made sexual noises with his mouth, and before I could open the door to my truck, he grabbed it. I turned to look up at him, and that put us inches apart—if not centimeters.

"If you ever need a couple of dollars, Shoney, you call me. I'll be more than willing to give you whatever you need."

"Thanks, Daxx, but I'm good." My climbing up into my truck caused me to take a step backwards and bump him in the process. I unintentionally put the ass on him, but when he palmed it, I jumped. He smiled. "Nigga, have you lost your mind, Daxx?"

"No."

Once Daxx was walking towards his car and I was behind the locked doors of my truck, I exhaled, tried to figure out what the hell had just happened, and tried my best to shake the thought that Daxx had just come on to me. Whether it was drugs or alcohol, that had never happened before, and I was feeling some type of way.

When I did walk into the resource center, the first person I locked eyes with was Alyssa, and she was looking me over as if I was someone she hadn't seen before, causing me to look at myself over.

"Dizzy ass been fucking all night."

I turned, saw September smiling at me, and threw my finger to my mouth. Silencing her with an expression was something that hadn't been done yet, and that was apparently something I'd forgotten. "Will you shut up, Sept? I overslept," I told her while making my way to my cubicle.

Sept followed. "You probably slept with the dick in your mouth too, huh?"

I sat my bag next to my desk, shook my head, and fell into my seat. It was then I remembered the bag Daxx had given me, as well as the encounter between us. I told her, "Girl, let me tell you what ya ex, Daxx, did this morning." I knew those words would get her to be quiet. At least for a minute, anyways.

"It ain't going to surprise me, I'm sure."

Just as September took a seat across from my desk, Mr. Dillan walked by, saw me, and took a couple steps backwards. "Ms. Wilson—I mean, Mrs. Edwards." Mr. Dillan was probably the only one that addressed me by my married name, and I smiled at that, but the rest that came out of his mouth had me wanting to slap him with both hands.

"Mrs. Edwards, I'm going to have to document your tardiness."

"Mr. Dillan, I had a long night, and I overslept," I tried to explain as best I could without putting him too far in my business.

"She got some dick last night, and this morning, Mr. Dillan."

I closed my eyes and lowered my head. That damn Sept was something I'd never be.

"You do seem to be glowing, Mrs. Edwards, but I'm still going to have to give you a write-up. Imagine me allowing everyone to come and go as they please."

I looked from him to Sept, because I knew those weren't the words he was meaning to say. Not to me. "Are you serious, Mr. Dillan?" After all the shit I'd done for his punk ass.

"Sorry, Mrs. Edwards, but…"

Instead of finishing his statement, he walked off, and I damn near walked out. I told Sept, "You hear that shit, Sept?'

"I got him. Don't even sweat that shit, Shoney."

"Like I've got to be here or something." I pushed myself back into my seat. Our co-worker approached with a look of concern but really wanted to know what was said.

"He ain't tripping, is he, Shoney?"

I was normally that rational-minded co-worker that played cool with everybody, but today, I wasn't feeling rational or cool, and when Sept went a fool, I didn't even as much blink.

"Yeah, he tripping, and I'm about to trip too if you don't get out of her face, with your knock-kneed ass."

We watched our co-worker walk back to her station. It did feel good to have someone who had my back, even if she was sure to get us in some shit. "I know they are going to get together and kick your ass one day, Sept."

"They'll find their asses at the bottom of Lake Ray Hubbard fucking with me."

And for the first time, I really did believe her. September might have been a pretty woman with a brightness about her, but there was also a grey and black area she walked in from time to time. I told her, “Look at what Daxx dropped off this morning.” I slid the bag to her with my foot, watched her rifle through the contents, and look up with a smile that told me I shouldn’t have.

“Bitch, you know how to make a bitch’s day,” she told me.

“And guess what else he gave me?” I leaned forward, made sure no one was lurking, and told her, “An invitation to make some money on the side. This was right before he squeezed my ass.”

Sept looked at me with wide eyes. “He squeezed your ass?”

“Will you shut up, Sept? I told *you.* I didn’t stand on the deck and scream it to everyone.”

“That nigga squeezed your ass, Shoney?”

“It damn near felt like the nigga used both hands too,” I told her before adding, “I really think he was drunk, or high on that shit.”

“Dirty ass nigga trying to fuck you, Shoney.”

I shook my head. “Naw, he was just high,” I told her, having never come to that conclusion.

“High, my ass, Shoney. But if we play this shit right, we can hit him for a nice piece of change.”

When thinking of Sept’s words, I had to say she might have seen what I couldn’t and didn’t want to. Raylon and Daxx had been friends since forever—done some of everything together, and now that I was so-called “wifey material,” it was very well possible that he wanted what Raylon called his own. Then, too, we might have been tripping.

***

Raylon

I was hoping to catch Asia before she left for work, and when seeing her barely walking out of the house when I pulled up, I knew I was going to have to do some explaining, as well as some promising. When I was entertaining Cindy at the Shack, Asia called, and by the time I’d made it home, it was late, and Shoney needed to be tended to. I’d lied to her about being home earlier, but one thing led to another, and before I knew it, I was behind on time. Cindy stayed on my mind for most of the night, and the moment Shoney entered the shower with me, I couldn't think of anyone else but the chocolate goddess of a woman driving the maroon Bentley Continental.

"Asia." I parked, climbed out of the truck, and made my way to where she was standing.

"What happened to you last night, Raylon?"

Asia was so beautiful to me, but her only flaw was that she was light complected. I loved me a chocolate woman, and there was no comparison when it came to the two. Plus, that was not her decision to be made that way when it came to who and where I'd end up. Asia had her own, and that was what attracted me to her in the first place. That, and the fact that I could stash shit at her house without having to worry about it coming up short or missing. In exchange for the favors she gave, I made sure bills were paid, as well as any other perks accommodated.

"You know how shit gets when you lose track of time," I told her.

Asia was one of those women who had a nigga that was stationed overseas and called herself saving the pussy for him. She gave me head, let me fuck her in the ass, and didn't mind wrapping her voluptuous titties around the dick, but I couldn't penetrate that pussy for shit, and believe me, I tried.

"Well, hopefully, you'll be able to come to me tonight." Asia kissed my lips, gripped my dick through my slacks, and bit her bottom lip.

"I'm sure we can make something happen," I told her before walking into her house and closing the door behind me.

I always took care of calls, checked calls, and packaged my work while Asia was at work. With me paying the bills, I had keys to both the house and the storage shed out back. This was where I came to get away at times and when she wasn't at work. It was here I was treated like a king. I phoned Cindy while making a mental note to call Daxx, so I could pick up that money for the buy-in.

***

Daxx

Brent was standing near the rear of the car lot when I pulled up. It was already understood that he'd ride with me to check on a couple of the spots. I needed him to see and know what was going on just in case I needed him to make a run or a stop. While on the way there, my mind kept going back to the encounter I had with Shoney. Raylon had told us so much about her that I couldn't help myself. Her shit was firm, and now her ass had me wanting to do more than I did. I knew she wouldn't tell, because she wasn't the one to start shit. Not like September. It might have been the drugs, but when seeing her chocolate ass in them tight ass jeans, all thoughts went out of the door, along with the fact that, that was my nigga's wife. Hell, Raylon was fucking so many hoes, there was no way he was doing Shoney the way she should have been done.

As soon as I climbed out of the truck, Brent walked towards me shaking his head.

"How was the date last night, crack head?"

"Perfect," I lied.

Not only did I offer Sheila some of the same dope I'd been selling, but I'd seen a guy there at the restaurant who owed me money. And despite her call for me to let him make it, I approached him, anyway. That led to words being exchanged and us being asked to leave in the middle of our meal. And instead of her letting me make it up to her, she climbed in her Range Rover and left. I called her three times last night and this morning, but she had yet to answer my calls. I wasn't trippin', though. Because I knew she'd come back around, especially if she wanted to get paid.

"That's good to hear. I was starting to worry."

"I told you I got this shit, nigga. You ready to hit the streets or what?"

I had to admit. Brent was making good with his promises when it came to the way he ran the business. All I needed for him to do now was just act hard on a hoe.

"Did you pay Sheila that money like we talked about?"

I shook my head. "Not yet. Me and her supposed to be getting together later on. I'm going to make sure she's straight, though. We had other things on our mind last night."

Brent and I made some rounds, picked up the money that was owed, and talked about future plans. He was wanting to open up another place of business, but as soon as he started talking about September's snake ass, I changed the subject.

"How much did you say that was?" I asked, talking 'bout the cash I'd just given him.

"This is $4,600."

"That's it?" I stopped, made a U-turn, and headed back to the spot we'd just left. "This motherfucker short again," I told him, having already come to the conclusion that something had to be done. It was bad enough that the motherfucker I caught up with last night was stalling me on the ends, but for these niggas to work in my spot and still short me? I had to make an example.

"You strapped?" Brent might have purchased a collection of guns, but he wasn't the type to carry them, and I needed for him to know that this was mandatory when dealing with this kind of shit.

"Yeah. It's at the shop, though."

I sighed, handed him my .357, and told him, "Just hold it for me right quick."

"What—what you 'bout to do, Daxx?"

"Nigga, bring your scary ass on. These niggas playing with our money. Next, they'll try to play with ya life." I reached into the back of the cabin, grabbed the wooden bat, and climbed out. I told him, "If a nigga so much as look wrong, you pop a cap in his ass."

I led Brent to the back where our workers were posted. The guys and women we passed were either scoring heroin, or trying to exchange something for it, and although I swallowed it at times, I still told them to make sure the money was right, because the way I ran the spots, it didn't matter if you made the quota. I made sure you got the same package every time. That's why I was tripping on the fact that money was coming up short. I gave them every opportunity to make the shit right.

I looked towards the youngsters that hustled out of the spot. "Y'all know this shit sort again, right?" By the way they cast glances at each other, I knew some shit was in the game. I looked to the one closest to me and said, "Isn't that your new F-150 outside?"

"Yeah."

"Give me your keys right quick." I stuffed them inside my pocket and told him, "When you niggas start getting my shit right, you'll get these keys back."

"Come on, Daxx. I—"

Before he could finish his lie, I swung on him, hitting him square in the chest with the bat, and as soon as he balled up and began coughing, I hit him in the back and legs. "You motherfuckers think this is a game!" I yelled at those in the room. "This ain't no motherfucking joke! This is a business, and you run the motherfucker like a business!" I hit him again.

"Daxx."

I looked towards Brent, saw the surprise in his eyes, and told them, "This motherfucker wanted me to kill one of you niggas, but I didn't. I've got love for y'all. I'm the one making sure you niggas still got a place to make shit happen." Since they rarely saw Brent, I made it as if he was the guy supplying the spot. I had them thinking that the big man himself had come to pay them a visit. "Get this shit right around here, because this is the last time I'll pay the debt." I gave Brent the keys to the youngster's truck and nodded towards the door.

Once outside, Brent handed me my pistol and held up the keys. "What am I supposed to do with these, nigga?"

"Take the truck to the detail shop and put it in one of the stalls. I'll give it back to him in a week or so."

"I can't believe you did that shit, Daxx. You could have really hurt that boy, man."

I smiled, nodded, and climbed into my truck. I told him, "It was either that, or let Rubberhead swing through this bitch."

We both knew what that meant, and instead of arguing, that nigga only climbed into the truck and pulled off. I pulled off as well. Now all I needed to do was make sure Rubber got back with our shipment safely.

Chapter Five

Shoney

I was just about to head back upstairs when I heard the beeping sound of our security system. Raylon wasn't expected until later that night, and when hearing his voice, I yelled, "Sept!" I ran half-way up the stairs, thought better of it, and ran back towards the foyer to short shop him.

"Shoney! Shoney!"

My heart pounded in my chest because there was no telling what he'd have done to either of us had he caught us in his safe. After leaving work, September and I raced to my house with the $60,000 so she'd have enough time to do her thing. The thing of it was that with it being so much money, I had to help her do the count, and that meant instead of me watching out—like I'd done many times before—I was sitting right alongside of her with a shit load of dollar bills. I just so happened to have gone downstairs to get a juice when I heard him entering.

"Shit."

"Hey, babe? What you doing? Working out?" he asked, seeing the perspiration forming over my brows and hearing my labored breathing.

I was glad that I stepped out of the jeans and blouse I wore to work and slid on a pair of full-length tights and a sports bra. Because if it wasn't for that, there was no way he'd have believed the lie I came up with.

"Yeah. Had to see what that new DVD I ordered was about."

Raylon smiled, grabbed me by the waist, and pulled me to him. He kissed my full lips. "Did Daxx swing by here this morning?"

One again, my heart was trying to find a way out of my chest. Did Daxx say anything? And if so, what was said? I'd been debating whether or not to bring up the matter, but Sept told me—made me promise that she'd handle it, and instead of answering what wasn't asked, I told him, "Yeah, he gave me a bag while I was on my way to work. It's up—" I caught myself because that's exactly where Sept was, and him walking up on her while she was going through the contents of his safe wasn't something I wanted to be a part of.

"What's up, pretty ass nigga?"

I closed my eyes and sighed when hearing Sept's voice behind me. I didn't know how she did it, but she was cool, calm, and collected under such pressure, and when seeing her walking from the kitchen with a fruit juice in her hand, I laughed.

"What you doing here, Sept? I know you ain't doing no working out." Raylon walked towards the kitchen, and I followed.

I looked back, gave Sept a quick glance to make sure everything was as it should have been, and walked towards the fridge. "You hungry, babe?"

"Naw. I just had to swing through and grab a few dollars. I'm on my way to OKC for a while."

"Babe, you know what happened last time you went there with drugs on you," I told him, having to say something to feel him out.

"Yeah, well, this is different. I'm going to see about a horse, babe."

I looked at Sept, and she only rolled her eyes. We both knew he was lying, but I wasn't about to be the one that exposed it. I simply replied, "What the hell are you going to do with a horse, Raylon?"

"That's where the game going these days, babe. Niggas buying horses, racing horses, and selling bloodlines."

Raylon was so confident in his spell that the game he spit seemed effortless and without thought. I didn't know shit about horses, but now that he'd mentioned them, I couldn't help but think about the money the bag contained, so I asked, "So, that's money inside that bag?"

"Yeah. That nigga trying to get in on the winnings. He knows I'm running a good pick."

"Let me put in on it then."

We both looked over at Sept—who was as serious as she could be. I frowned, and Raylon smiled.

"How much you talking about?" he asked her.

"I'll give you a grand."

Raylon laughed, shook his head, and told her, "Woman, a grand can't even buy the shit off the horse's ass. You might be out of your league on this one."

The minute Raylon headed up the stairs and was out of hearing, I whispered, "Did you close it back and clear the keypad, Sept?"

"I closed it, but I didn't do shit to the keypad."

"Dammit, Sept. I told—"

"Shoney! Shoney!"

The tone of Raylon's voice told me he knew what we'd just done. We were busted, and I knew it.

"Play the part, Shoney. Don't start that shit."

I rolled my eyes at September and headed for the stairs. "Here I come, babe." I slowly walked into our bedroom, expecting to see him standing in front of his opened safe, but instead, he was in his walk-in closet changing shirts.

"Babe, I don't know how long it's going to take me to get things straightened out up there, so I might not be home tonight." He then looked at me with an expression that had me thinking it was really my call, but when he pulled out a wad of bills and handed them to me, I knew I'd just been given my part off.

"Um, okay. Do you need me to ride with you?"

"Naw. I'm going to meet with a group of country motherfuckers, and ain't no telling what might pop off." To add to that, Raylon strapped on his shoulder holster and slid his newly bought .44 inside.

"Babe, you be careful." My concern came with the full understanding that he might have been lying his ass off, but still.

He then walked over to me, kissed my cheek, and reached for the sports coat I bought him just days ago. "I'll call you once I get there, and I'll call once I'm leaving."

With that, I walked Raylon downstairs and outside to his truck. He threw the bag Daxx had given me in the passenger's seat and climbed in himself. "I love you, babe. If this shit goes right, we're going to be sitting on a million, plus."

I smiled when seeing his smile. His enthusiasm would have normally excited me, but I'd been through this with Raylon before, and when all was said and done, it was some kind of excuse. And on top of that, there would always be a next time. I nodded, closed the door of the truck, and leaned up to meet his kiss.

"Just be careful, Raylon. And call me." It was sad that was all I could ask and more so expect.

***

Daxx

I continually checked the time on my watch because it was about time for me to hear from Raylon, anyway. I'd already dropped off the cash and was really wanting to hear if his wife had said anything about our interaction earlier. I had already told myself that if she did mention it, that I was going to deny the shit, and at least blame it on the drinks. I was yet to tell Raylon that I'd started back toting a little bit, but it was nothing like before, and there was nothing really to worry about when it came to it. I knew how to handle my business.

The minute I saw that it was Raylon trying to contact me, I hit me a line, handed the rolled bill to Rubberhead, and took the call. "You get that?" I asked, getting straight to the business.

"Yeah, I just left the house, and I'm on my way as we speak. What we look like with the spots?"

"Oh, we good. Me and Brent had to set an example earlier, but everything is everything now."

"Brent? What the hell he was doing at the spot?"

I ran down the event play by play, because I needed for him to see that I'd hardened my hand when it came to dealing with motherfuckers. He'd always been the one to not really sweat it if they came up a little short, but like I told him, brand-new trucks and cars should not be bought and our money was coming up short.

"You playing them too hard, Daxx. Those are workers. Not niggas we trying to run over."

"You just make sure you take care of that shit you got going on. I got this end." I completed the call with Raylon and smiled. Shoney hadn't told him anything about what we'd talked about. I personally knew how it was when women hid shit that should have mattered most from their men. I knew first hand when a bitch wanted to be handled. She might not have said it, but that's what she liked. Raylon had already told us how she liked to get 'worked on,' and how she liked when a nigga got aggressive. "Chocolate ass."

Rubber pushed the coke-filled tray towards me and said, "Don't start mixing that shit, Daxx."

"I don't even fuck with that heroin, Rubber." I did another two lines myself.

"I'm not talking about no dope, nigga. I'm talkin' about them thoughts you've been having about yo' nigga's wife. You can peel a few bills off of a stack, but when you fuck with a nigga's wife, everything else goes out of the window."

I listened to Rubber and knew this was the advice to take heed to, but Raylon didn't give a damn about Shoney, and I was aiming to see just how much she gave about him. "I'm not even thinking about that bitch, Rubber," I lied.

I was really debating whether or not to stop by the house a second time, and knowing he was about to be out of pocket for the rest of the day, now was as good of a time as any.

***

Shoney

"We good, girl. We good. That nigga didn't suspect shit."

I'd been pacing the room ever since Raylon pulled off, because despite him not saying anything, I knew his mind was in overdrive when it came to what me and Sept were doing. He knew I hadn't been working out, and evidence of that was when he went upstairs and got that money. He had to have seen that none of my workout equipment was out and his closet door was still slightly ajar. Raylon always placed things a certain way, and I was more than sure he noticed but chose not to say anything because of September's presence. Either that, or he'd wait until he got back before addressing it.

"I don't know about this shit anymore, Sept. Once he thinks about it, the first person he's going to fuck with is me. I—"

"Hell, Shoney. You know damn well that nigga ain't no 'bring it up later' type of motherfucker. His ass had some more shit on his mind, and if I know Raylon, it has everything to do with a bitch."

"He didn't take all of that money to give to no other woman, Sept. He might have been telling the truth for once." I said the words but couldn't believe them myself.

"And he damn sure ain't going to tell you when he's about to gamble all his money off. But let him tell it, his shipment came in today, so you know he ain't going to buy no damn drugs."

"We should have followed him, huh?" I stood, walked toward the bay window, and looked out at my front yard. Some shit like that was right up Sept's alley. I was sure.

"Let's go."

It sounded good, but we didn't have the slightest clue where he was headed, or where he'd end up. "And what if he ain't going to Oklahoma?"

"You put the tracker in his phone, didn't you?" Sept stood also, gave me her 'I know you didn't' expression, and fell back down onto the sectional.

"I put it in the last phone, but that nigga change phones all the time, Sept, and I just haven't had time to do it again," I told her, knowing different.

"With your lying ass. Shoney, if you had to save your own life right now, ya ass would have been dead. You've had plenty of chances to track that nigga's shit. His phone, his truck, his ass, and everything else the nigga got. Your black ass ain't trying to catch that nigga."

Sept kicked as if she'd just found out she'd failed an open-book test. As if that was the one and only way we'd run up on Raylon doing some shit he didn't have any business doing.

Her tantrum made me smile. I told her, "Fuck Raylon."

"And fuck you too, with your lying ass. You make me sick, Shoney." Sept threw the huge pillow next to her at me. She then dug into her bag, pulled out a stack of bills, and held them up. She said, "That's why I took this from his safe."

I dove at her. "Give me that, Sept!" She spun from under me and ran. "I thought you said fuck Raylon?" Instead of chasing what wouldn't be caught, I fell onto the sectional and laughed.

We both just laughed.

***

Raylon

Before calling Shoney upstairs and letting her know that I might not be home tonight, I popped a Cialis pill. Cindy and I had talked a good while, and it was already understood that we'd meet up and do what grown folks did. I made a couple of stops, collected a few dollars, and made my way to meet Cindy.

When pulling into the lot of the LaQuinta Inn Hotel, I searched for her maroon Bentley, as well as the cars of people who I knew hung out in this part of town. I was no stranger to the jack game, and if that's what this all turned out to be, they weren't going to get what they thought. I'd placed the money into the compartment where I normally kept my gun, and the cops hadn't even found that place yet, so I knew they wouldn't.

Not seeing anything familiar or suspect, I climbed out and hit the stairs. She'd given me both directions and the room number, and before I could knock, the door swung open. I jumped when seeing her standing there naked. Her chocolate skin shining like new money. I looked her over, my eyes stopping at the areolas of her breasts. Large, round chocolate nipples pointed up at me, and they were erect already.

"I started to think you wasn't going to show, so I began the party without you."

"You should have known better than that," I told her before looking past her to see who else was here. I walked past Cindy, half-turned to see her naked ass. It looked tight and heavy. Just like Shoney's. I nodded, saw that she was alone, and turned to face her.

"I've been waiting to fuck you, Raylon. I've heard so much about you."

"Is that right?"

Cindy was the most aggressive woman I'd met, because as soon as she closed and locked the door behind me, she grabbed the buckle of my belt and pulled me to her. She bit my bottom lip, kneeled down, and began unfastening my zipper. I looked towards the bathroom door when hearing the toilet flush, and before I could blink, I was pushed forcefully onto the bed, and the light-skin woman I'd seen at the Shack walked out. She only wore some red lace panties.

"So, you've finally decided to join us?"

For that split second, images of Shoney and September came to mind when thinking of them at the house earlier. I couldn't shake the fact that I walked in on something I shouldn't have. I asked them, "Is this what $50,000 gets me?"

"This part ain't even about the money. Matter of fact, we are going to pay you."

I fell back, watched Cindy pull my dick out and begin massaging it, then watched as the light-skin chick massaged Cindy's breasts, hips, and ass. I wasn't going to make it home tonight. I wasn't going to even try. Both Shoney and Asia would have to go on about their night, because these two were my night and day, and as always, the night came first.

Chapter Six

Shoney

I'd waited for Raylon's call all night, hoping he'd at least be considerate enough to do so. I got up early and tried to get me a twenty-minute run on my treadmill, but ended up standing under the steaming waters of my shower, crying. I just couldn't understand the shit I was putting up with.

By the time I walked into the resource building, September was already there, and being that I was early myself, that was a first. Everything was going fine until Mr. Dillan had the nerve to stop by my cubicle talking about writing me up for some shit that happened days ago.

"Are you fucking kidding me, Mr. Dillan?" I stood, grabbed a stack of files from my desk, and slammed them back down.

"Just calm down, Mrs. Edwards. Just—"

"Naw, motherfucker." I began gathering my shit. "You know what? Fuck you, and fuck this job!" I watched Mr. Dillan's expression. I'd never talked to him like that, but it was long overdue. When looking at him, I couldn't help but see the rest of my co-workers looking on in amazement and September standing behind Mr. Dillan with a smile plastered across her face. That alone told me that I was tripping.

"I would like to have a word with you in my office, Mrs. Edwards."

As if putting me in my place, he had the nerve to walk off. I reached for my stapler and would have thrown it at his ass if so many people weren't in the way. "Punk ass!" I replaced the stapler, took a deep breath, and collapsed into my recliner. I couldn't believe what I'd just done.

"That nigga must not have come home last night?"

I wasn't feeling like entertaining Sept in the least, because all she was doing was pissing me off also. I told her, "This ain't got shit to do with Raylon, Sept." I pointed towards our supervisor's office and said, "I bend over backwards for that motherfucker, go out of my way to make sure shit is right around here, and he pull up on me like that. Fuck him, Sept!"

"See, this the way you need to be talking to Raylon's punk ass. I know that nigga shitted on you last night, and we both know he ain't laying up under no damn horse."

I rolled my eyes, took me another deep breath, and closed my eyes. I had to get out of here. "I quit."

"Hold on. Let me get my shit."

Before I could reason with Sept, she spun on her heels and went to log out on her computer. I didn't say shit about her doing the same thing as me, but it was apparent.

"Come on, so I can tell Mr. Dillan to suck my dick too."

"Sept, just because I'm—"

"Fuck that shit, Shoney."

Sept grabbed my bag and led me into Mr. Dillan's office. I was just about to curse his ass out some more when Sept told him, "We're going on break, Mr. Dillan. We'll be back later."

"But you've just got here, Ms. Hassan."

September pulled me in the direction of the door and called over her shoulder, "We're going on break, Mr. Dillan!"

Like always, Sept grabbed the keys to my M6 and drove. Moments later, she pulled into the lot of the Subway sandwich shop and parked. "Why are we eating here?" I asked, knowing she didn't do Subway.

"Business, Shoney. Business."

Before sitting at the small table, I ordered a chicken club, a small bag of Sun Chips, and one chocolate chip cookie. Yeah, today would be a cheat day for me. Sept, on the other hand, ordered several chocolate chip cookies and a fountain drink, and had the nerve to say, "Let me taste that, Shoney."

"If you want one, order you one," I told her before taking my first bite.

"A bitch get tight when she can't wake up to no dick."

"Fuck you, Sept."

"You probably would right about now."

Sept placed her phone on the table between us and smiled. I didn't. And when seeing her cross her leg over the other, I knew she was about to begin her counseling session, and I was about to be the victim. "Don't start, Sept. Don't even start."

***

Raylon

The continual ringing of the phone on the nightstand next to me pulled me from the dream I was having. The ceiling alone told me that I wasn't in my own bed, and when finally taking notice of my surroundings and the pounding headache I had, I jumped, snatched the phone up, and groggily asked, "What's up?"

"I was instructed to give you a wakeup call this morning," said the soft voice on the other end.

I looked from where I laid towards the bathroom door. "Cindy?" It was then that I noticed the note and a stack of bills. "Um, yeah, okay," I told her before hanging up. I looked at my phone, saw that it was 10:40 AM, and reached for the small note. It read:

Raylon,

Thanks for a wonderful night. Sorry I didn't wake you before leaving—you seemed to have needed the rest. I look forward to hearing from you soon.

-Cindy

Cindy had left half of the money I'd lost days before next to the panties she'd worn. I smiled. The bitch had her shit together in a major way. I was always the one to encourage Shoney to do something with her time and money, but she was content with being a housewife. It wasn't that I had a problem with it, but she could have been doing more.

After dressing and making a few calls, I sat on the edge of the bed, scrolling through text after text, and decided to phone Daxx. It was about time for Rubberhead's dope fiend ass to return with my shit, and I didn't need it in his hands too long. I thought about Cindy and Carmen, saw two opened condom wrappers, and shook my head. I couldn't really remember shit, and what I did remember had me wanting to see Cindy again.

Daxx answered on the second ring. "What's up, Raylon?"

"How's it looking on that end?" I asked before standing and walking over to where I could look down over the parking lot of the hotel.

"Everything is everything on this end. They want $5,000 apiece."

That's bullshit!" I fingered the bills Cindy had left and did a count of all that was in my safe. "That's bullshit, Daxx."

"I promised them the bonus, Raylon."

"Then you pay it, nigga. I'm not giving them dope fiend ass niggas nothing else."

I ended the call with Daxx and grabbed my keys. I still had to deliver the $50,000 to the boys in the OKC.

***

Daxx

Instead of taking the call personally, I pressed speaker. I had a feeling that Raylon was going to be tripping with the bonus I promised Rubber and Gunz, and I needed them niggas to know that it wasn't me that didn't approve of it. Raylon had made it known many times before that we were throwing money away when it came to the two, but because of me, I kept them in the loop, as well as paid. I looked over at Rubber and shrugged.

"Sounds to me like ya boy needs to be reminded that he can't make money without us making the moves."

I leaned forward, reached for the rolled bill Rubber held, and cut me a nice thick line of the 'winter white.' I told him, "This nigga must have lost a bet or something and need the cash."

"We might need to pay that bitch of his a visit."

"She ain't got shit to do with this, Rubber. If some shit just so happens to fall back on her, then that's going to be his doing. Not ours."

"You getting soft, Daxx."

I pulled the line, pinched my nose, and threw my head back. Images of Karen's mangled and disfigured face came into view. Despite what Raylon did and didn't do, Shoney didn't deserve no shit like that. "Soft or not, Shoney is off limits as far as that shit goes." I had other things in mind for Shoney's chocolate ass.

***

September

I sat and listened to Shoney whine as if she'd just found out the nigga she'd been dying to fuck whipped out a skinny ass dick or something. My girl was pissed the fuck off. She'd been pissed before, but never had she been the one to take it out on other people. Especially our supervisor. I wished I'd recorded that shit. The only thing I didn't like was the way Shoney kept saying the shit that she was pissed at was over the bitch that was fucking her husband.

"I'm telling you, Sept. When I catch up with him and some bitch together, I'm going to kick her ass. I promise you that."

I checked my phone, reached for one of the cookies I'd bought, and shook my head. I asked, "So, ya dirty dick ass husband just get to walk off, huh?"

"And I'll deal with his ass when we get home."

"Oh, so that's how you do? Rip your clothes off and let him fuck the shit out of you while promising to never do the shit again? That's how you deal with him, huh?"

"Hell no. I'm going to hurt his ass too. I'm tired of playing this down ass bitch while he's down every bitch that smiles at him."

"Then you give the pussy up. You stop coming home and start lying about the shit you do. Walk in the house with your hair all over your head and looking as if you just got fucked, and when the nigga demands to see ya panties, you make sure them hoes still wet."

Since she was tired of the shit he did, I might as well have told her how to get back. Then, too, we'd had this exact conversation many times, and each time, she always found a reason not to.

"You know I'm not going to do all that shit, Sept. I just want him to know that enough is enough."

"Well, hold that thought right quick," I told her when seeing Jacoby pull up, driving a new 550 Benz.

"Who is that?"

I stood when seeing him enter and smiled when he was making his way to us. He was a handsome brother, but what I was more interested in what was the bag he held over his left shoulder and the contents in it. "Hey. You're looking good today," I told him, stroking the ego I knew he had.

"And you as well, September. And you?" He looked towards Shoney. "My friend has been asking about you for the longest."

"She was just asking about him right before you—"

"No, I wasn't. Don't pay her any mind, Jacoby. You already know how Sept is."

There was no use in me telling her that his friend had just opened a business in Dallas, nor was there a need for me to tell her that he'd taken in over a quarter of a million dollars in the last three months. These were the niggas I now hustled with, and they were also the reason Shoney had something nice to put back for herself.

"Well, sorry I can't stay. I have a meeting to attend to myself."

"Don't forget you have to take us out, Jacoby." I looked over at Shoney because she was known to fuck something good off. I watched her with narrowed eyes.

"Yeah, yeah. Just let me know when, Sept. You know I got you," he replied before subtly changing the bag he was carrying with the one I sat on the table. I should have known Shoney was on to us, despite her looking elsewhere when he did. And to let me know that she was paying absolute attention, she nodded.

"What was that all about?"

I placed the bag next to my foot and told her, "You, me, and the shit we've got going on. You ready to go back to work, or what?" I changed subjects because I didn't need to add to the stress she was already under, and giving her the game from the root would have definitely had her ready to break.

"Don't be trying to change the subject, Sept."

"Are you ready or not? We've been here for over an hour," I told her.

"Man, fuck that job, Sept. I'm tired of them hoes, anyway. I can be at home doing me instead of fucking with them."

I reminded Shoney of the play we were running. Told her that it wouldn't be long before we were onto our next chapter and grabbed the bag I was given. I told her, "Don't worry about Mr. Dillan, Shoney. I got him. He just be trying to save face. He knows he's a bitch in my book."

"Well, the way he's been acting lately, he got me fucked up."

I felt for my girl. Not because of the shit she was dealing with at work, but because she was choosing not to deal with the shit she had at home. I just didn't want her to be one of them women that lived in regret and refused to leave. And leave broke at that. If and when Raylon did kick her to the curb, she'd be alright, and that's what I was making sure of.

"When we walk back up in there, make sure you apologize to Mr. Dillan, and if he wants his dick sucked, you clown that motherfucker," I told her before climbing behind the wheel of her M6.

"Bitch, you got me fucked up. I might have to suck his dick, but I ain't apologizing for shit." She laughed.

Knowing we were that much closer to our goal, I laughed as well. Shoney might never admit it, but she knew I was right. And she knew I always had her best interest at heart.

***

Brent

I met with Sheila at the bank, took care of that business, and stopped to buy Sept a little something-something from the Vantage Show Warehouse. I was more than sure she'd love the pairs of boots I bought. I even bought her a couple of nice silk scarfs I liked.

I noticed the sky-blue unmarked car even before pulling in the lot, because I pretty much knew the surrounding area, and to see the addition now, it was obvious. I prayed like hell it wasn't the feds, because I'd just taken money from Sheila to put up in the safe I kept in the rear of the shop. The money I kept on hand was used to give loans, buy cars, and pay for sudden expenses when it came to the lot. Instead of parking in my designated spot, I pulled around by the service center and called one of my workers over. "Hey!"

"Hey, boss, what's up?"

I nodded and asked, "How long has the sky-blue car been parked across the street?"

"You talking about the Lincoln?"

I frowned. He'd noticed it also. "Yeah, I see you've noticed as well."

"Those guys have been waiting for you in the lobby for the past half hour."

"Guys? What they want with me? Are they cops?"

"Sure looks like it. I know they're strapped, though."

I watched him head inside to answer the summons on the intercom. There was always the thought of cops walking in and taking everything I'd worked for, but them coming this soon was something I never anticipated. "Damn," I told myself before climbing out of my car and heading inside myself. If they were coming, I had no choice but to get shit over with.

The two guys immediately stood when seeing me, and that told me they knew exactly who they were needing to see. I then waved them into my office, took a seat behind my desk, and leaned forward. "How may I help you guys, Officer?" There was no need in beating around the bush.

"Um, well, we have reason to believe you're hosting a stolen truck on the premises and wanted to speak to you about it."

I sat up. "Stolen truck? I have the titles, registration, invoices, and everything else for the automobiles I have here." I then logged in just in case they wanted to verify anything, and as soon as I punched in the last digit of my user password, I thought about the truck Daxx had me take to the detail shop.

"Um, you mind if we take a look around, sir?"

I stood, extended my arm towards the rest of the building, and led them out. They might not have found the truck at this particular location, but I did know exactly which one they were referring to. I was going to kick Daxx's ass if I got the chance to. "Right this way, fellas."

Chapter Seven

Shoney

For an entire week, Raylon had been constantly fucking up. The nigga was disappearing during the day, acting strange as hell at night, and there were even days when he didn't come home at all. Him using Brent or Daxx for cover-ups wasn't happening anymore, because for whatever reasons, they were mad at his ass too. But to-day was the day it all came to a head.

We were supposed to have gone out last night to support a cou-ple of women I knew that were doing great things in the fitness world, and I really wanted to be at that event with my husband. The nigga had called talking about having to make a quick run out of town, but it was evident he was lying because not even twenty minutes later when I called, he was at the exact same location, be-cause the same television show I was watching could be heard in the background. But let him tell it, he was on the highway thirty miles from wherever it was he spoke of needing to go.

And for him to still not be where he was supposed to be this early in the morning, I knew he had to have been with some bitch. As always, September was the person I called when I need to vent and, it was her that came running when I felt myself spiraling out of control. She stopped by early this morning to let me know that she'd be out of pocket for most of the day, and that it was and would be beneficial to the plan we'd put in play. I already knew she was just saying the shit because she didn't want to hear about the shit I was screaming about Raylon, but once she saw me disheveled, because of having cried my eyes out all night, she knew I was at the end of my rope.

"I'm telling you, Shoney, just don't do nothing stupid."

I looked from Sept towards the window overlooking our drive-way. Raylon had called over an hour ago talking about he was around the corner, and the nigga still hadn't showed. "This nigga got me fucked up, Sept. I know he's been with some bitch, and the shit has got to stop. Or I'm beating that bitch's ass."

"I wish you could hear yourself right now, Shoney. What the fuck she got to do with your man fucking over you? A bitch just trying to get in where she fit in, and you mad at that. You crazy."

"Bitches know he's married, and they just need to leave the nigga alone," I told her before making my way over to the fridge. I grabbed me a protein shake and handed Sept one for herself.

"I don't want no damn shake, Shoney. I have some shit I need to do, but I need to know that you ain't going to do no stupid shit. We've come too far for you to fuck it all off because you ain't waking up to no dick, girl."

No sooner than I'd replaced the shake she'd declined and closed the fridge door, Raylon's truck pulled into our drive. I was ready to kick his ass. I pulled my hair back into a messy ponytail, kicked off my house shoes, and went to meet him at the door.

"Shoney! Shoney! If that nigga hit you back, we're going to have to kill him. You ready for that?"

I stopped, looked over at Sept, saw her 'in all seriousness' demeanor, and closed my eyes. I'd been waiting to slap the shit out of Raylon all day and night, and for me to be denied this channel of release, it took a lot out of me. I told her, "That just might be what we need to do."

"Think I'm playing if you want to, Shoney."

When seeing Sept reach in her bag and pull out the black .380 handgun, my mouth fell open. "Sept, where—what in the hell are you doing with that?" I mean, my girl was known for carrying a box cutter, but this was some shit I needed to know more about.

"I'll tell you about it later, but right now, you need to promise me that we ain't about to kill this nigga."

My eyes followed Sept's hand as she replaced the gun back into the side pocket of the Ralph Lauren handbag she had.

"Promise."

I nodded my understanding, because she was talking literally, and I was just saying some shit to make my mouth move.

"Shoney! Babe, where you at?"

Instead of going to meet the voice of the man I couldn't stand to see at the moment, I walked back towards my kitchen. I told him, "I'm in the kitchen, babe."

"I've got a surprise for you, babe."

I would have usually greeted him with a nice kiss and a compliment, but I only leaned over the island counter and cupped the glass I was drinking from. My mouth moved, but the words just wouldn't come, and I hated myself for that. Raylon walked up behind me, wrapped his arms around my waist, and leaned over. He kissed my neck, my ear, and pressed his middle against my ass. I tried to move from under him, trying to defend myself against the weakness he used against me.

"Where were you, Raylon? I called and called and—"

"I've been on my best shit, babe, and the last thing I need you doing is worrying about the moves I be making. I don't like you worrying like that, babe."

I looked towards Sept and saw the disappointment in her posture, because this was the way it started every time. I turned, put my back against the counter, and looked up at him. "Seriously, Raylon?"

"Here."

I knew it was going to be some shit, but when he pulled out the jewelry box and presented me with an Audemars Piguet watch, I closed my eyes. I'd been wanting this watch for a minute.

He pulled my chin towards him and kissed my lips. "You know I love you, right?"

"Um, I'm about to head out so you two can talk," said Sept.

Raylon and I looked towards Sept, but he was the first to speak.

"Don't let me stop what y'all got going. I just need to jump in this shower right quick. I've been on the road all night," said Raylon.

My first mind was to follow Raylon upstairs and bombard him with the questions I'd been wanting to ask all night, but I, instead, just stood there and watched him disappear down the hall. I looked down at the watch a second time, closed the box, and sat it on the counter.

"You straight or what?"

"Yeah, yeah. I'm just going to let that nigga do him," I told her before covering my face with my hands.

"Walk me out right quick. When I get back, I'm going to show you something."

Sept and I were standing alongside the door of her coupe when the thought came. I looked up towards the window facing us and made my way to my husband's truck. When seeing that it was locked, I walked around the driver's side, punched in the four-digit code, and climbed in. I inhaled the familiar fragrance, looked for any sign that told the tale, and there it was. In the center console were two Styrofoam cups. One with a straw, and one without. I grabbed it and climbed out. I handed it to Sept, wiped at the tears that threatened to fall from my eyes, and placed both hands on my hips.

"What's this?"

With both eyes closed, it was seen as clear as day. I, again, wiped at the tears welling in my eyes and told her, "Since when did Raylon start wearing lipstick?"

"Stupid ass nigga." My girl regarded me with pleading eyes, threw the cup down the driveway, and reached for me.

"I'm good. Naw, I'm good, Sept." I pulled back from her. "Go on and take care of your business. Let me take care of mine."

After she reluctantly climbed into her car and pulled off, I stood for a couple of seconds, thought of some shit I'd seen on one of them police shows, and made my way back inside. I headed straight for the kitchen, grabbed a butcher's knife, and made my way upstairs, all the while telling myself, "Yeah, let me take care of mine."

***

Daxx

The ride from the Westside took a little longer than it should have because I was dealing with more than a couple of dealers wanting more than I'd been giving them. It was agreed that Raylon would do the pickups on the Northside, but he'd already called talking about he'd make the stop later, and I was really trying to see where the count was at. I didn't know what Raylon had going on, but he was reneging on motherfuckers that were loyal to him and fucking around in the OKC with some niggas we knew little to nothing about.

I'd just left the Bernel apartment complex when I was cut off at the light by some guy driving a late-model Chrysler. I'd seen the same car on a couple of occasions and paid it no mind, thinking he either lived in the complex or wanted to get in on a hustle. I pulled into the driveway and parked when seeing him do the same. I jumped out. "Man, what the fuck is wrong with you?" I asked the words but thought something else when seeing another guy approach from the passenger's side of the same car. Both men wore masks but only one brandished a weapon.

I slowly backed up.

"Naw, don't run off now, nigga!"

I watched as he approached me. Being that we were under the overpass and on the back street, not too many people were able to see what was taking place. And the ones who did, they were getting out of the way.

"Whoa, whoa, whoa," I coaxed him with raised hands. "Y'all know who I am?" I ran these spots, and if they weren't about to kill me, they were dead men. It was obvious that they were still teenagers because of the move they were making. Old heads wouldn't have needed a mask because it wouldn't have mattered if you saw them or not.

"What he got in there?"

I glanced back at the direction the passenger went. He was sitting in the driver's seat going through my shit. It was then that I wished I had a compartment to stash both money and drugs. One thing I knew was that they had to have known I was holding at the moment, because as soon as he found the kilo and a half of cocaine, he held it up and smiled, revealing the diamond grill in his mouth. What stuck out the most was that his fronts were on the bottom, and the diamonds were either red or orange.

I asked them, “Is that what this is all about?”

“Shut your bitch ass up, nigga! Check that nigga pockets, blood!”

“Let me make it, youngster. I can put you and your team on,” I told him, knowing what greed did to young minds. I also knew by their lingo that they were blood.

“Let you make it? Let you make it? Matter of fact, take the car. Fuck that nigga!”

I stood there and smiled. It had been a while since I’d been robbed, and it was definitely a wakeup call given. If only them niggas had waited until I’d made a few more rounds, they’d have been sitting on more than just a kilo and half of cocaine and $4,200.

“Young ass niggas is dead,” I told myself before pulling out my phone and dialing Brent’s number. The guys must have been new at the shit because they let me keep my phone and most of all, my life.

***

Brent

“Hold up, hold up. They did what?”

Daxx’s call came just as I was pulling into the lot of the detail shop. If it wasn’t one thing, it was another with this nigga. We’d already had words about him having me house a stolen truck at the building we called a business. Not only that, but he’d been fucking over Sheila, and I was the one making it right on that end. Daxx had started back using that shit and couldn’t see the way things were shifting around us. Now for him to call talking about some young niggas had robbed him, it only made me more suspicious of the shit he’d been doing.

“Just come get me, nigga. I’m going to deal with that shit later.”

“Have you called Raylon yet?” I asked, because if he had, and Raylon wasn’t even taking the time to get involved, I wasn’t going to either.

"Naw, that nigga been on some more shit, and I didn't feel like hearing it this morning. My mind is fucked up, and I just need to get right."

By getting right, I knew exactly what he meant and how he intended to do it. I shook my head. "What they get you for, nigga?"

"Some crumbs. Them dumb ass niggas got themselves killed behind some crumbs."

When I did finally pull into view, Daxx was leaned against the wall of the service station with one foot planted back on the wall. If I was the cops, I would have sworn he was posted with a pocket filled with rocks. Amid all the people that came and went, Daxx was the freshest, and everyone seemed to have something to say to him. I watched him climbed into the SUV I'd recently bought.

"For you to have just gotten robbed, you looking real nice, nigga." I knew what robbery victims looked like, and it didn't look like this nigga got dragged at all.

"Some young ass niggas got what they wanted and left." Daxx shrugged, thumbed through his phone, and made calls.

I could tell he was high, and that alone was the reason I wasn't believing a word he said.

"Looks as if I'm going to have to buy me another car after all, huh?"

I only shrugged. Hell, I had plenty to choose from. Getting him some wheels was nothing. Getting him off the drugs was the challenge.

"Have you paid Sheila yet?"

"Man, fuck that bitch. That hoe ain't talking about shit."

For the rest of the ride, I glanced over at Daxx and knew he was traveling down a dark road. This was the same road that landed him in prison, and I wasn't going to become a passenger. I wasn't about to let this nigga bring me down, and I damn sure wasn't going to let him get me killed.

"You need to slow down, Daxx. I've seen this side of you before, man."

"Nigga, you tripping. I got this. This kind of shit happens in this game, Brent. You've got to roll with it or get rolled by it."

"Well, just be careful, nigga. We got a lot riding on each other, and if one slips, we all might just fall."

I watched Daxx nod his agreement but knew he was only doing so to appease me. That was something he did when he didn't want to discuss nothing. And I knew exactly why. It was time I called Raylon and we all talked about this shit. It was time to either put this shit back together, or pull it apart.

***

Shoney

For more than fifteen minutes, I stood outside of the bathroom door thinking and listening. Thinking of my next moves while listening to Raylon go off on whoever it was on the other end of the phone. I no longer wiped at the tears that one time threatened to fall. I was now wiping perspiration from my forehead. Not only was I heartbroken, but I was mad as hell. I looked down at the knife in my hand and closed my eyes. I knew I wasn't about to kill Raylon, but I wanted him to know I would.

I wanted to place the blade to his neck and scare the shit out of him. I wanted to make him promise that he'd stop the lies, the cheating, the gambling, and damn near everything else that kept him from coming home to me at night, but I'd already done that, and he still found a way to put his foot in my ass. Always did.

I jumped when I heard the door open and squeezed the handle of the knife when Raylon walked out. Naked.

"Shoney, babe, what you got going on?"

I turned my face so he couldn't see that I'd been crying.

"Bae, what's wrong?"

For a brief second, I looked up at my husband, saw the concern in his expression, and looked away. My heart began double-timing because this was it. "Who is she, Raylon?"

"That was Brent, babe. He was telling me—"

I cut him off and saw his eye drop to the knife I was squeezing. I said, "I'm talking about this bitch you're putting before me."

"Shoney, you tripping now. That's why you got a knife?"

Raylon and I locked eyes. I searched his features, and his went back to the knife. He walked towards the bed. I followed. "I know you've been with some bitch, Raylon. I know you."

I watched the beads of water trickle down Raylon's back onto his tight ass. I walked directly behind him. He turned to face me.

"You going to use that thing, Shoney?"

"Who is she, Ray!" I grabbed the knife tighter, felt myself shifting from leg to leg.

"You want to kill me now, babe?" Raylon opened both his arms, daring me.

"I want to know who this bitch is, Raylon." The tears found their way back, and Raylon wiped at them before they fell. I let him.

"Ain't no other woman, Shoney. And it damn sure ain't no man. I'm doing all the shit I can to make sure we're straight, babe. I love you. I married you. You mean the world to me, Shoney. I can't believe you want to kill me."

Raylon sat on the edge of the bed and looked up at me with the saddest expression I ever saw him make. He was hurt. Maybe just as hurt as I was.

"I can't keep doing this shit, Raylon. It's either me or her, and I'm serious," I told him.

My husband pulled me to him. Buried his face in my stomach and wrapped his arms around me. I couldn't pull away—didn't want to.

"You mean the world to me, Shoney, and you know this."

I looked towards the ceiling to keep from crying and shook my head because I could go no further. This was as far as I'd gotten in my demands that he'd be a better husband, and the nigga was melting under me. I told him, "I love you, Raylon. I'm the one that's been there since day one. I don't deserve to be treated like this, Raylon. You don't come home for days at a time, and when you do, it's evident that you've been with…" I used the back of my hand to wipe my face.

Instead of reaching for the knife, Raylon stood, pulled me to him, and embraced me with one of the warmest hugs ever. He kissed my forehead, pulled my face to his, and began sucking my lips.

"Stop, Raylon."

"This is my pussy. You gonna keep me from my pussy, babe?"

I felt him pull at the shirt I was wearing and stepped back. He was not about to use his dick. I wasn't going to let him. Hell, I couldn't. "No, Ray."

Before I could push him away, he spun me in one quick motion, and before I knew it, I was laying on the bed, and he was using his body to pin me down. I struggled under him, remembered the knife I was holding, and tried to raise it, but he'd clasped both of my wrists with his left hand and pulled my shirt above my head with this right. He used my shirt to bind both of my hands.

"Move, Raylon!" I bucked under him.

"You gonna make me take this pussy, Shoney, huh?"

With my hands pinned above my head and his weight on me, he yanked the tights I was wearing down, taking the sides of my panties with it. Raylon then leaned down and began biting my neck hard.

"Raise that ass up, Shoney. Raise it up."

I raised slightly, hoping he'd stop biting my neck, but he didn't. I felt him push my panties down with his foot and with his knees, he wedged them between mine and spread me apart. I gasped when he entered me, and it surprised me at how wet I'd gotten. Raylon slid his dick right in and began a slow thrust. Using only half the length of it, he thrust in and out, in and out. I raised my ass so he could go deeper. I wanted—needed him deeper.

"Take this pussy, babe. Please," I begged. Raylon's tongue filled my mouth while his arms and hands reached under me and squeezed my ass. I lifted my legs higher, bent my knees to give him full access, and wrapped my arms around his neck. I still gripped the knife I was holding, but instead of placing it to his neck, I bit him and told him, "Fuck me, Raylon." My breathing was ragged, my rhythm off, but I threw the pussy as hard as I could. I made him chase it, and as soon as I felt him hit the bottom of lil' mama, I locked my legs around him. I needed him to stay there forever. "Fuck this pussy, babe. Fuck this pussy," I coached him.

There was no way she was fucking him the way I was. No damn way.

Chapter Eight

Shoney

Today, I'd taken off work so I could take care of some things around the house. I also wanted to do something special for Raylon, 'cause for the past three days, the nigga had been treating me like a queen. The nigga catered to me in grand fashion, and if I would have known me pulling a knife on him would have rewarded me in such a way, I'd have been done it. Not only was Raylon coming home at night, showering me with gifts, giving me hot oil massages, and cooking full-course meals, I was put to sleep with the dick and awakened by it also. The shit was perfect, but like all good things, it slowly came to an end.

This morning before he left, I sucked his dick and made him promise to be home earlier than 8 PM, because I was going to have a nice surprise for him. And like always, he agreed. I'd been beaming for the past few days and would not have had it any other way when it came to the way he was making me feel.

I went out and bought a $2,300 projector, four huge Italian leather recliners, and a cedar oak wet bar for his theater room. That way, he'd be able to entertain his guests at home instead of having to go elsewhere. I knew it wasn't going to lock him down or keep him from going out. I just wanted to be here when they did arrive. Not only that, but I wanted to have things set up for when he did come home.

When hearing the doorbell ring, I snatched my towel from the handle of my treadmill, wiped my forehead, and made my way downstairs. "Just a minute!" I yelled, hearing the bell ring once more. Through the opaque windows of our front door, I could see a person, and thinking it was the delivery man, I swung the door open and smiled.

"Um, I'm looking for a Raylon Edwards."

I then looked past him and saw the UPS Parcel truck behind him. I nodded. "Yes, he lives here," I told him before wiping my forehead a second time. The guy had to have been in his early twenties, but he was cute, had a nice build, and seemed to be respectful. I looked him over with thoughts I knew I shouldn't have been thinking. I had to literally shake my head when wondering how thick his dick was. I made eye contact with him briefly and followed him to my breasts. The sports bra I wore was slightly moistened, and my nipples were semi-erect. I smiled at him.

"I have a delivery for him, and I need a signature." He then handed me his clipboard.

"Come in, come in," I urged him, remembering my manners. "Would you like a beverage or anything?"

"I'm good," he responded.

I walked towards the kitchen and half-turned, saw him watching my ass. Once again, I smiled. I was on my work out, and I knew I was looking nice.

My thoughts went to some shit I saw on TV, and I couldn't shake the shit. I caught myself looking down at the bulge in his uniform pants while I signed for the package. Thought about the many times where young guys made stops to older women's houses, only to find them alone and depressed, and ended up naked with their dicks in some lonely woman's mouth, or better. I thought this was what he was thinking. Those thoughts were interrupted when seeing the name of the sender.

"Cindy West? Who the fuck is that?" I asked aloud.

"Beats me, ma'am. I'm just the delivery guy."

After being handed the small box, I saw the youngster out and walked it to the counter in the kitchen.

"Cindy West?"

I continually asked myself if I'd ever heard the name before but couldn't place it. I flipped the box over, hoping to see anything familiar, but saw nothing. It was killing me not to rip the box open, but I had to do the right thing. Well, I wanted to do the right thing, and giving Raylon his privacy, along with the benefit of the doubt, would have been the thing to do. I walked away from the box, got halfway up the stairs, and heard the doorbell again. I rushed back down thinking it was the same guy, realizing a mistake was made, but instead, it was the delivery guys I'd been expecting. Once everything was signed for and I'd shown them where to set up, I found myself back in the kitchen looking down at the small box.

"Cindy West?"

I called September at work.

***

Brent

As always, Sheila was a welcomed distraction and just like her arrival at the barbershop, the guys at either the lot or the detail shop made sure she had a pleasant stay. Although I no longer worked at the barbershop, she still stopped by every now and again to entertain Mr. Williams and the rest of the guys. Sheila was a very likable person and a damn good friend.

"And what did he have to say about that?" I asked her in reference to what Mr. Williams said about me acquiring the property across the street for September.

"You already know he and the rest of the guys had more than two cents for the collection plate."

"Them niggas ain't going to ever change."

My mind drifted to the fact that for years, some of the same guys had been coming, doing the same shit, working the same jobs, talking about the same things and were just going nowhere. Now that I was making moves with and without my boots, I promised myself I wasn't going back. And that's where the conversation headed with me and Sheila.

"It's good to see you're actually doing something different," she told me while crossing one leg over the other.

"Yeah, thanks to you. If it hadn't been for you coming into my life, I don't know what I'd be doing." The minute the words came out, they seemed to echo through the office, and I was actually able to hear what was said. I told her, "I mean, as far as—"

"I know what you mean, Brent. My meals come with knives and forks now."

I smiled when hearing her retort. I nodded also and said, “I don’t see how that nigga let you go.”

“Have you ever thought about me letting him go? That may have been the case.”

I looked from Sheila towards the window. It had always been the thought of mine that it was her that couldn’t keep a man, but when watching the way things went with her and Daxx, perceptions changed. Sheila had a vision not many guys saw for themselves, and she had goals she wasn’t ‘bout to compromise for. She and September were so much alike and because of her, I was able to better understand my own girl. And because of Sept, I was understanding of the things she’d been through. “But still. When a nigga got a good woman that’s about something other than herself, he should do whatever it takes to keep her. This is just how I feel.” I stood, walked around to the drawer of my desk, pulled out some files, and handed them to her. “In five years, I want to own at least one more establishment and be all the way legit.”

“Then I suggest you find better business partners.”

I knew who and what she was referring to, and I also knew she’d been seeing the exact same things when it came to Daxx. “This isn’t all for nothing, Sheila, so believe me when I tell you steps are being made. Me and the guys are meeting up this weekend, and we’re going to discuss some shit.”

“Well, good for you, Brent. Good for you.”

I thought about the conversation I had with Sept recently. I asked if she ever thought about settling down and starting a family, and to hear her say she had on many occasions, I felt like there were changes I had to make. September was looking for security, stability, and trust, and she wasn’t depending on a nigga to provide it for her. She did play a game when it came to relationships, but it was more so done to protect the emotions she’d end up developing for the person.

I made sure I continued to show her that I was all in when it came to her and whatever she wanted to do. I knew Sept had been hurt in the past, but that was a subject she chose to never talk about, and I didn’t pressure her. It didn’t take digging up bones to uncover a person's past, and Sheila was able to explain that to me. She also told me that in order to build a future with Sept, I'd have to show her that I was building one for myself.

I walked back around to where she sat and told her, "It's time to put all this other shit to the side. I've got money in the bank, two places of business, and a hell of an accountant that made it possible." I pulled her up from her seat and gave her a hug.

"It took all of this to get a hug out of you, Brent?" Sheila laughed.

"I guess September's finally rubbing off on me."

I walked Sheila out to her truck with a renewed sense of understanding. The first thing I'd do was tell the guys that I was out of the shit they had going on, and the second thing I was going to do was let my girl know I was ready for that next step. It was about time we started a family of our own.

***

Daxx

Finding the youngsters that robbed me didn't take long at all, because just like many of the other niggas that fell in the game, they didn't know how to sit on their work, and apparently, floating wasn't something they knew about. That was when you traveled to other cities and states to hit licks—not where you lay your head.

"So, what's the plan, Daxx?"

Rubberhead, Gunz, and I had been posted on the block across from the hole-in-the-wall pool hall watching the comings and goings of both hustlers and addicts, and with a $50 bill, we were able to confirm just who ran the spot and what it was they were selling. These guys apparently rocked the entire kilo and half and were going rock for rock. There was no quantity sold at this location, and from what we could gather, there was no other. I liked the fact that these guys were trying to make the most out of their win, but they'd robbed the wrong motherfucker, and I couldn't let it go unanswered.

"I'm going to suffocate that punk ass nigga that called the shots, and as far as the diamond-wearing cat, I'm going to see just how much dope he can handle." I pulled the heroin-filled syringe from the bag I was carrying and placed it on the dashboard. When seeing Rubberhead cringe, I knew it was more than enough to kill a horse.

"Good, 'cause I didn't plan on leaving my trademark so close to home," said Gunz.

"Y'all just sit back and enjoy the ride. Hell, we might even find out some more shit from these clowns."

***

Raylon

I'd been texting Cindy for the last few days because of the shit Shoney had going on. Asia was on my ass for having not shown up for our date night, and I was really needing a break. One thing I liked about Cindy was that she knew the position and played her part to the "T." She understood me having a wife at home, as well as a side piece. To my surprise, she knew more about me than I thought. Much more.

"Come out here, Raylon."

Cindy and I had checked into the same hotel we'd met at the last time we were together. She had a thing for balconies, and by the way she made sure we kept things both professional and cordial while in OKC, I had a feeling she was involved with someone else as well. Someone other than the light-complected woman we enjoyed days ago.

"Pretty nice view," I told her from where I stood.

We were on the ninth floor on the Northside of the building, which overlooked the pool and the visitation parking. I slid up behind her, wrapped my arms around her shoulders, and kissed her neck. Cindy was a bit shorter than Shoney, wore a short-styled hairdo, and was chocolate—just like I loved my women. She wasn't as thick as Shoney, but she was nice with slightly bowed legs. Her chinky eyes and button nose were evidence of her mixed heritage, but her body screamed she was black in every way.

"I want you to fuck me right here."

"You want me to bend you over the ledge too?" I was just joking when I made the statement, but it seemed to amuse her.

"Yeah, but don't drop me, Raylon."

I watched as she climbed on the balcony rail and turned to face me. Her legs spread, and the prettiest pussy I'd ever seen greeted me. I inhaled her scent and stood. I positioned myself between her and circled my left arm around her waist. Cindy's pussy stayed hot and wet, but if I had to choose between her and Shoney? My wife would win, hands down. It was just something about Cindy I couldn't get past, and I had planned on staying around until I found out what it was.

"Ouu, Raylon, you feel so good inside of me."

"You like that?" I teased Cindy with long, slow strokes while she placed her legs around me. I watched her expressions and changed my angle when she shifted, and sped up the pace when she called herself throwing it back. My wife, at times, acted as if she was fucking me, and the shit drove me crazy.

"I love this. I see why your wife be tripping when you don't come home."

I half laughed and positioned myself to where I could penetrate her deeper. That was one thing about Cindy. She couldn't take the dick like Shoney. I told her, "Turn around." I glanced down at my dick and noticed she came at least once, and that made my dick harder. "Spread that ass, babe." I knelt again, but this time, I pushed my tongue into her ass. She jumped.

"Shit, Raylon!"

I fucked Cindy right at sixteen minutes straight before I came. She made sure I shot my load in there, and to show me how nasty she was, she pushed the shit back out and tasted it. Cindy was nasty as fuck, and that might have been the reason I couldn't get enough of her.

"Are you going to get that?"

I looked back towards the suite at my ringing phone. I knew it was Shoney checking to see where I was and what I was doing, and I didn't feel like lying, so I just shook my head.

“Remind me to never get married.” She laughed before making her way to the shower.

I followed.

Chapter Nine

September

"Just open the damn box, Shoney. Damn!"

What I really wanted to do was find the bitch who'd sent it in the first place, because it wasn't like I found out my husband had mailed a bitch something behind my back. Then there was the issue about me giving Raylon both the benefit of the doubt and some kind of privacy. I told her, "I'm going to respect his privacy, Sept. I—"

"I, my ass, Shoney. Y'all married. Ain't no privacy."

I lifted the box for the hundredth time it seemed, trying to gauge the contents by its weight, and sat it back down. I looked out of the window towards our driveway to make sure Raylon wasn't pulling up. What angered me was that whoever the bitch was knew my address and felt it was cool to do some shit like this. It was always that I was the one at home when a delivery was to arrive, and I'd be the one to intercept the mail that came to the address. So, for whoever she was to send a package here, she had to have known that I would get it.

"You think Raylon's doing this shit to see what I'd do?"

"Don't start that white girl shit, Shoney. You know damn well that ain't the case. This Cindy bitch thinks she got herself a lick and is trying to let it be known."

I listened to Sept's perspective of the game, because she was as scandalous as they came, and I might not have said it all the time, but she was spot on for the most part. A scandalous bitch knew what another scandalous bitch would do and why.

"I dun went out and bought all this shit for him, and he has some bitch sending shit to my house."

"Open the box, Shoney, or don't call me no more."

I finally broke. I tore into the box, all the while looking out of the window for Raylon. "Cologne," I told her. "It's a bottle of cologne, Sept."

"Cologne?"

"Yep, some expensive cologne too."

"Well, there you have it. The bitch's name is Cindy, and she's fucking your husband."

I thought about some of the things Raylon said and couldn't help but remember back in the days when one of my co-workers called himself buying me a bottle of perfume. White Diamonds, matter of fact. Raylon made sure he paid the guy a visit at work, and after that day—no more perfume.

"Maybe she's just a woman that likes him. Remember when—"

"Bye, Shoney. I've got shit to do. I don't have time to be playing stupid. Just remember what I said while you over there so-called remembering shit."

After hanging up with Sept, I sat the bottle of cologne on the counter and shook my head. Was I tripping over nothing? Should I even ask my husband about the shit, or should I just leave the shit alone? Hell, he had been doing better, and I didn't want to give him any reason to feel as if I was not trusting him. I was just about to replace the bottle back in the box when I saw what looked to be card. A very small card. It read *Thanks* and was signed with a fucking kiss. A set of lips—thick lips—caused all the shit I was feeling just days ago to come back. I picked up my phone to call Sept back but ended up placing it face down on the counter.

I told myself, "I should have given the mail guy some pussy."

Maybe that would have evened the score. Maybe that would have made the shit right. Once again, some shit Sept said came to mind. What if I'd given the pussy up and Raylon found out? What if?

***

Raylon

From the bed to the balcony, and from the balcony to the shower, I chased Cindy with the dick. As soon as I got her to where I could finish the pussy, she'd think of another area of the hotel suite, and another position. She'd cleaned the both of us while we showered, even asked if Shoney did some of the shit she did and acted as if she had to do it better. I turned Cindy to where she could place her foot on the soap stoop and held onto the railing above.

"Stick that ass out, Cindy."

I slapped her sudded ass on both cheeks until she complied. I had to squat to get up under her, but once I did, each stroke lifted her. The sound of slapping flesh filled the bathroom, and the sight of her twisted face had me fucking her harder. I held Cindy's waist with both hands while pumping her. I grunted with each pound.

"Ughhhh!!!"

"Take this dick, babe. Stick that ass out," I told her when seeing her reach back to slow my strokes.

"I can't take it like that, Ray. I can't— "

She'd been teasing me with the pussy from the beginning, and I was going to make her take what I had to give. I grabbed her wrists and pulled them behind her back. I kept pounding, kept grunting, and each time my dick hit the bottom of her pussy, it continued to lift her.

"Raylon, please!" she begged.

When feeling myself about to cum, I released her wrists, stepped back, and squeezed my dick at the base. Cindy hurried and turned, got on her knees, and took me into her mouth. She pushed my hands aside and took me as far as she could.

Once again, I grabbed for the railing above, closed my eyes as tight as I could, and froze. "Aghhh, shit!" I released and pulled away, but that only fueled her more.

She then pulled my balls up to the side and began sucking underneath them.

"Oh, you taste so good, Raylon. Nuts taste like honey roasted almonds."

Cindy milked me for all I had and was still licking 'em when the dick went limp. She pulled out of the shower, led me to the toilet, and smiled.

"We forgot about the toilet, Ray."

I more so collapsed when I did sit, and when she knelt before me and started sucking the dick again, I only shook my head. To my surprise, it didn't take long at all for me to regain a throbbing erection, and it didn't take her any time to find a position she had not tried yet.

"Let me ride that dick while you watch this ass, Raylon." Cindy climbed on me backwards, leaned forward so I could see the penetration, and so she could control the depth, and looked back to me. "Do she do it like this, babe?"

While Cindy chased her nut, I thought about my wife and all the shit I'd been telling her for the past few days. No matter who they were or what they did, not many would compare to my chocolate ass wife. And now that she'd lost weight and had been working out, she was making it hard for the next bitch. But like all niggas, the best was never enough.

***

Daxx

Once the traffic had died down a bit, Rubberhead, Gunz, and I made it out to the trap. I'd slipped into an old jogger, and I had on a worn ball cap and a pair of shades. Rubber and Gunz were looking like their old selves. We hardly raised a brow as we walked up to the door and knocked.

"Y'all got some flipping fifties?" I asked, knowing how it was to hear that more than a dime or two was about to be sold.

"Come in, come in," said the familiar voice.

I made sure I held out the folded bill while entering. It didn't surprise me to see the two guys that robbed me and a couple more dope fiends sitting around the nearly empty room. I spied the sawed-off gauge on the side of the couch, as well as the .38 revolver on the table where the dope was being displayed.

"Unfold that shit," the guy told me, apparently having been got before.

Right as he reached for the bill, I pulled the cap from my head and removed the shades I was wearing. I smiled. "It was fifty dollars that led them to you," I told him before pulling the gun I was carrying.

"If you plan on living, get your asses out, right now," Rubberhead told the two dope heads.

"Not you, youngster," I told the guy that rifled through my pockets and took my car just days ago. I looked back toward the shot caller. "Didn't expect to see me so soon, did you?"

"Say, man. We were just doing what someone told us to do," he said while throwing his hands up.

I pulled the string from my pocket and nodded at Rubberhead, who then slapped the grilled-out youngster with the barrel of the pistol he had. We all watched as blood shot from his face onto the wall.

"Please, man. I didn't have nothing to do with it. Please!"

Once Rubber had him tied to the chair, I crossed the room, strapped the ligature on his left arm, and asked him, "Where's my car, punk ass nigga?!"

"They chopped it, man! Please!" He squirmed when seeing the filled syringe.

"Come on, Old School. Please, man."

As soon as I caught a vein, I pressed the needle into his arm and filled it with the potent drug. Tears fell from his eyes, and a muffled scream came from behind the hand Rubber used to cover his mouth with. It only took seconds for his eyes to roll back and foam to form at the corners of his mouth. I then looked towards his friend. "Shot Caller."

"The rest of the work and the money in the bathroom, man, I swear."

I laughed, looked over at Rubber, who was still holding the convulsing body of the youngster, and told him, "This dick sucking ass nigga think I want some dope and money."

"A damn fool he is," said Rubber.

I pulled the black plastic bag from my pocket, popped it open, and asked him, "How'd you know what I was holding the other day?"

"Mellow and them told me, man. They said you kept work and money."

"Mellow? Who the fuck is Mellow?" I asked.

"He's the nigga you stretched out at one of your spots last week. Everybody calls him Low."

"Oh, yeah?"

I knew exactly who Low was and had been wondering when I'd see him again. Ever since that day at the spot, he'd been MIA. The truck I took from him belonged to his mother, and she was the one who called the cops and had them searching for it at the lot. It was because of that nigga that Brent was flexing, and because of him, these niggas got killed. I was going to make it my business to catch up with Mellow as soon as I could.

Knowing I wasn't about to make the same mistakes he'd made, the shot caller went for the revolver on the table. While I held the bag over his head, Rubber restrained him from the back.

"Suck that shit, nigga!" I told him when seeing the bag being damn near swallowed in his attempt to breath. I looked up towards the door when it opened. Gunz peeked his head inside.

"Time's up, niggas."

When feeling the body go limp and smelling the shit that was running down his leg, I let him go. I took the cash from the sack he had on the other side of the table and nodded for Rubber to get the stash from the bathroom. My workers were turning against me, and before I let some shit like that pop off, a whole bunch of motherfuckers would come up either dead or missing.

***

September

It didn't surprise me one bit when hearing that one of my coworkers had posted some shit about Shoney being arrested again. Hell, it didn't surprise me that they even had her name in their mouths. These were the same motherfuckers that smiled in my girl's face, complimented her for her transformation, and went to her when it was some shit they wanted her to discuss with Mr. Dillan. I stood, looked around for that loose-mouth bitch, Alyssa, then asked my other messy ass co-worker, “Where that bitch at?”

They couldn’t wait for this moment to start some shit, and like Shoney said, they’d probably wait until she wasn’t around to do it, but I wasn’t trippin’ on these broke ass hoes. I was about that life. I wasn’t that bitch that went and watched no *Love and Hip Hop* and thought posting some fake ass shit on my site made me gangster.

“I think she was called to Mr. Dillan’s office,” said Mrs. Messy.

If they thought I was scared of Mr. Dillan’s dick sucking ass, they had another thing coming, and that was the reason why I made my way there. Shoney was the best thing that happened to these bitches, and as fate would have it, it was her absence that set the shit off.

I stormed in Mr. Dillan’s office, saw Alyssa standing there with a fake ass smile plastered on her face, and walked over and slapped the shit out of her ass. She tried to swing back, but I side-stepped her and bust her right in her shit.

“Say something about her now, bitch! Say that bullshit now!”

Alyssa didn’t back down, and I wasn’t expecting her to. She threw a slew of wild punches and ended up hitting me in my face.

“Ladies, will you please—” Mr. Dillan cried.

“Whoop that bitch, Alyssa! Whoop that hoe!” someone screamed from behind me.

I grabbed the stapler from Mr. Dillan’s desk and popped Alyssa upside her head about six times before she balled up and began begging Mr. Dillan to help her.

“Get out the way, Mr. Dillan!”

“Ms. Hassan, will you please calm down! Please!”

When seeing him shield Alyssa as best as he could, I turned to the crowd that’d formed at the office door and asked, “Who told that bitch to beat my ass?” No one said shit. “Scary ass, bitch, you do it! Whoever you are!” I told them before heading back to my cubicle and gathering my shit. “You hoes got September Hassan fucked up!”

It was right around quitting time, anyway, so I wasn’t all the way out of line, and besides, Mr. Dillan told me just days ago that he wished someone would kick her ass. If he meant anything by it or not, he told the right motherfucker. Knowing I had to check on my girl and give her the rundown, I phoned her and told her to meet me at the headquarters. It was about time I sped this shit up.

Chapter Ten

Raylon

The minute I walked into Asia's house, she was on me. I'd been avoiding her for the past few days, and I knew what she wanted, as well as needed. It was always here where I came to wind down, and the king's treatment definitely did the job.

"Where are you headed?" I asked when seeing her dressed as if she was either coming or going.

"Nowhere now."

Asia closed the door behind me and followed me into the living area. I knew she was about to try some stunt at making sure I spent the night, but I was going to have to take her up on that later. There were things I had to deal with, and fighting with Shoney again wasn't one of them.

"Let me find out you were going to meet up with some nigga," I told her before taking the beer she offered me.

"Really, Raylon?" Asia walked around, kneeled between my legs, and began undoing the buckle of my belt. "Let me show you who I've been trying to catch up with," she said before massaging my dick with both hands.

"Before you start some shit, Asia, I want you to know that I'm not going to be able to stay the night. Me and Shoney already had a fight about the shit, and I do have to meet up with the guys early."

I watched as Asia pulled my dick from my boxers and kissed it. She pulled my balls up and began sucking them.

"Mmm, this dick is so good to me."

"I'm serious, Asia."

"Well, there goes the thought of you getting some of this pussy tonight."

I laughed. She'd always played that card when it came to me bending to her will, because I'd been trying to get the pussy for a minute. Asia knew how bad I wanted to fuck her, and because of that, it was hard to tell when she was serious or not.

"Yeah, right."

"Babe, I need some money," she told me while licking around the head of my dick. She pushed her long black hair to the side, tilted her head, and took both my balls into her mouth. "Mmmmmm."

"How much you need?"

Asia got as much as she wanted, and I liked the fact that she didn't abuse the shit. I paid the bills and some because she was always willing to hold and store what Shoney didn't. I might have kept large quantities of money at the house, but when it came to my work, it was here I came. I adjusted myself so she could get the full dick.

"I need $1,300 so I can get me a new laptop. I also want one of them new Galaxy S10E."

As soon as Asia finished sucking my dick, she cleaned me up and climbed onto the couch behind me. She then began massaging my neck and shoulders. She was really trying to put a nigga to sleep. I smiled, tilted my head to give her access, and closed my eyes.

"When are you going back to Reynosa?"

"I hope never, but them niggas Daxx got going for me want more money for the trip, so now I'm having to do something different."

"What about the drop that just came? How much did they bring this time?"

"Somehow, they brought nine. I only sent enough for eight, and because they know this, I'm having to pay them for the contents of the package instead of the charter."

"Sounds like they trying to make it worth their while."

I placed my head onto Asia's lap, felt her lean in to kiss me, and told her, "What they doing is fucking off more of my shit."

"Are these the guys you spoke of being behind the murders not long ago?"

I raised slightly, faced Asia, and frowned. I told her, "So, you know I can't trust them with too much of my business."

"Yeah, you do have things to attend to." She laughed.

"But you know what, though? They ain't no damn fools. It ain't like I'm some walk-up. I can get just as deadly as they can."

"I know you can, Raylon. Hopefully, you won't have to do any of that again."

I checked the time on my watch, texted Shoney, and pushed my phone into my pocket. Seeing me about to stand, Asia jumped from the couch and ran towards her room. She knew what time it was.

"Don't run now. You know you got this coming," I told her before stepping out of my slacks and chasing after her.

Despite her calling herself punishing me by not giving up that ass, I knew she'd be naked in less than a couple of minutes. Hell, as much cash as I was leaving her with, it was expected.

***

Shoney

After walking around the house for an hour thinking of what I should and shouldn't do, I grabbed my keys and found myself zipping up and down the residential streets. And once I was sure the cops had seen me pass a second time, I hurried to go to the apartment I shared with Sept. She called me twice already to make sure I'd be there. She also said something about some drama at work.

I was in the kitchen responding to a text from Raylon when she walked in and threw her purse across the chair by the door. My girl's hair was looking disheveled, and I smiled when thinking of her doing what I'd just done. Now that we were able to drive faster cars ourselves, we made sure we enjoyed them whenever we could. My smiled faded the closer she got.

"How long have you been here?"

I shrugged, adjusted myself on the stool, and said, "About ten or fifteen minutes."

"Were the cops parked out front when you pulled up?"

"What happened to your face, Sept?" I noticed the small knot on her forehead, and the darkened welts on her cheek and neck. "What did you do, September?"

"I hope them hoes ain't called the cops and told them where I lived."

"Who?! What are you talking about?!" I stood, regarding Sept with raised brows, because she'd definitely done something.

Just a day ago, she'd shown me a gun, and today, she came home looking to have been fighting. I followed her towards the hall.

"Make sure that door locked, Shoney. I'm going to tell you all about it."

I stopped, looked back towards the door, and headed that way. If the cops were looking for my girl, they weren't about to just walk in, and I damn sure wasn't about to tell them she was here.

"I don't know what you're up to, Sept, but you—" I jumped when seeing her standing behind me when I did turn.

The sinister grin, along with red eyes, not only had me leaning away from her, but her appearance had me about to unlock the door and walk out myself. I looked down towards her hand, expecting to see the same gun she'd shown me the day before, but instead, she held two old beat-up backpacks.

"Come here, right quick."

I followed. Slowly.

"I had to dig in that hoe Alyssa's ass today," she told me when finding her favorite spot on the sofa.

"What happened? Did y'all get caught or what?"

"I beat that bitch's ass. That's what happened, and Mr. Dillan had to save that bitch."

"Oh my gosh, Sept. Are you crazy? I bet you it was behind some bullshit, too."

"That messy ass bitch was spreading rumors about you getting locked back up because you didn't come to work and some more shit. I was already having a bad day, so I got off in her ass to make it right."

I sat and listened to Sept run things down from beginning to end and even had to question her a few times. Because I knew how she got when she ended up in some shit, and none of it was her fault. I'd always been the one to tell Sept fuck what them hoes say. The shit wasn't that serious. What it really was, was that she'd been wanting to have it out with that woman long before now, and now that I wasn't there to stop it, she saw that as the perfect opportunity to do so. She could say what she wanted to say, as many times as she wanted, but we both knew the real honest to GOD truth.

"I just hope that bitch didn't call the cops on me."

"Sept, you hit the woman with a stapler multiple times, embarrassed the shit out of her—I'm sure—and you think she ain't going to call the cops. Really?"

"Well, take a few pictures of my face and neck, then. Just in case the bitch do go running to the police."

Sept threw me her phone and began posing as if she was in a police lineup or something. I took a couple of photos of her face and several more of the welts and scratches on her neck before handing the phone back to her. She then picked up one of the backpacks and began pouring the contents on the smoked-glass table between us.

"Oh, shit, Sept. What the hell did you do?"

I couldn't believe the amount of money she was dumping out before me. I knew that girl kept some cash on hand, but this was on a whole other level.

"It's what *we* did. This is all *your* money, Shoney. I'm not out here playing with these niggas."

For the next thirty minutes, I paced back and forth from the living area to the front door. I'd looked out of the peephole a hundred times, it seemed, because I knew someone was about to run up in here on us. I'd seen Raylon with a shit load of money many of times, but never had I been told it was all mine. I didn't even care about looking in the second backpack, because when she told me that there was $100,000 in that one alone, my mind took me to places I'd never imagined before.

"I don't know about the hit, Sept. You didn't tell me this part."

"That's because I didn't want you tripping like you're tripping right now. If you would have known we were bleeding your man like this, you would have been closed the curtains, and I need you to perform, Shoney. These niggas running through some major paper, and I'll be damned if we don't get ours."

"And Brent has been the one putting you up on game when it comes to the money that's coming and going?" I asked her.

I knew Brent worshiped the ground she walked on, but he wasn't crazy enough to turn against Raylon. They'd been friends forever.

"Once Brent starts thinking the pussy is his, he tells me everything. And when I do put this motherfucker on him, I get paid, Shoney: money, game, knowledge, and whatever else I feel can be useful."

"September Hassan, you are crazy." I stopped pacing, looked down at the stacks of cash between us, and smiled. I still didn't know what all she was doing, but one thing I did know was that I wasn't going to stop her. I was going to ride, and whatever cliff she wanted to drive off of, I was going to throw my hands up and enjoy it. "Just don't get me killed, Sept."

Chapter Eleven

Brent

After leaving Sheila, I went ahead and stopped by my girl's apartment because there was something I wanted to discuss with her. She also told me she'd be headed there after work because she and Shoney had to go over a few things.

Them disappearing and ending up in somebody's galleria or boutique was always a possibility, and I wanted to get at her before that became likely.

I parked next to Shoney's M6, grabbed the envelope containing the $2,500 I promised her, and climbed out. She was going to trip when I told her about the beauty supply store, and when thinking about the things Sheila and I discussed, I was debating whether or not to let her in on the plans I was putting into effect. I rang the doorbell and looked back towards the parking lot. I had to get my girl into a nice home soon. The complex she lived in was nice, but this was nowhere to plant roots.

"Who is it?"

"It's me, Shoney," I called out.

"Just a minute, Brent."

I frowned when hearing her reply. I, again, looked back towards the parking area to see if there were any unfamiliar cars. I was hoping like hell there weren't any guys inside. "Do I need to come back later?" I asked.

Right then, the door swung open, and Shoney stood there with a silly smile etched across her face. "What's up, Brent?"

I nodded at Shoney and walked past her. "What are y'all up to now?"

"Girl talk. You know it's always something when it comes to your girl."

"Yeah, tell me about it."

September walked through the hallway entrance just as I was about to sit down. I immediately noticed the knot on her head, and the welts on her cheek.

"Damn, babe. What the hell happened to you?" I, again, looked over at Shoney.

"Nigga, don't be looking at me. I didn't even go to work today."

"Are you alright, Sept? You need me to get you anything?" I walked over to examine her face. It didn't surprise me that she'd been fighting. But fighting at work—that was another story.

"I'm good, I'm good. What are you doing here? That's the question we need to be answering."

"Well, I've got some things I need to talk to you about, and I know how you are once you get in traffic." I handed her the envelope and smiled when she thumbed through the bills and nodded.

"Let me get my ass out of here before I witness some shit I'll be having nightmares about."

I looked towards Shoney and said, "Naw, you good. I need your input on something, anyway."

September sat in her usual seat and pulled her feet under her. I reached for them. "And what are we talking about this time?"

"Us."

"Aw, shit. I really need to leave now."

Shoney stood, grabbed her phone, and headed for the door.

I stopped her. "I need you to holla at Raylon for me," I told her.

"What's up with this *us* shit, nigga. Fuck Raylon."

"That's the thing. I'm trying to build something with Sept, and I'm leaving all that other shit alone. I have two legit businesses now, and I can help her better than I could without them."

"Build something like what?"

I gently massaged Sept's foot before saying, "I want to move her into a nice home like you and Raylon's. I can help her do whatever it is she's longed to do, and I want to settle down while we're still able to." Shoney smiled, and September rolled her eyes. I continued. "I know you've heard the shit before, but I want to show you."

"Nigga, whatever you've been smoking got you on some more shit, and the motherfucker you been smoking it with got to be still there."

"I'm serious, Sept. And to show you I'm not just talking, I'm going to transfer $100,000 into whatever account, so you can do whatever you want to do."

The look Shoney gave Sept told me that they'd been plotting up on something, and when Sept pulled her feet from my lap and stood, I knew I was about to get put in the middle of whatever it was they were scheming.

"Give it to me in cash."

"Huh?"

"Cash. I want it in cash."

"But—Sheila told me that—"

"I don't give a damn what Sheila talking about. I can do more with the cash right now."

My eyes went from September to Shoney, because something wasn't being said. "What are y'all up to?"

"Nigga, are you going to give it to me or not?"

"Not if you're going to get in trouble with it, Sept."

"I'm going to need most of it for bail because I fucked a bitch up at work, and I'm more than sure she's going to call the cops and file a fake ass report."

And judging by the bruises on her face and neck, there was some truth in the confession. Hell, there was always truth in whatever September said.

"And with the rest you're going to have to retain a good lawyer?" I asked.

"Yeah, yeah. A real good one at that."

***

Daxx

The guys and I pulled up to the spot where the majority of the youngsters worked and climbed out. I dapped up a few of my workers while making my way inside. Today was a new day, and I had a new look when it came to the bullshit I was seeing. This spot had been short for the last few weeks, but after the spectacle I made with "Low," things had gotten straightened out real nice.

"What's up, hustlers?" I greeted the room with an approving nod. I could tell a couple of them had reserve about themselves, but my beef wasn't with them. Yet.

"Hey, boss. What's up on your end?"

"Man, I'm trying to find Low. I owe that nigga an apology, and I'm just trying to make it right. You niggas have been out here going through it, trying to make it happen, and I was on some bull-shit the other day." I looked around the room, gauged the expressions they wore, and asked, "Where that nigga hiding?"

"I ain't seen him in a week or so," said one guy.

"He ain't coming back around here," said another I knew to be real tight with him.

I'd have to make sure I spoke with him privately. Because he wasn't about to snitch, either.

"That nigga be at his baby momma house over there in Creek Point," he continued.

By the way they looked at him, it was apparent he'd given up something he shouldn't have, and to reward him for it, I dug into my pocket and handed him $1,000.

"Well, tell him to get at me. Me and him need to sit down and talk. By the way, is he alright?"

"Yeah, that nigga will live. You fractured his ribs and bruised his spine, but that nigga alright."

The ride to the Creek Point Apartments was a quiet one, because we were all dealing with thoughts of our own. Rubber and Gunz were thinking of a lick they could put together for themselves, and I was thinking of a way to tear this young nigga apart. The thought of letting him make it and acting as if nothing ever happened did cross my mind, but then that would only encourage them niggas to try some shit like that again, and the next time, they might not make the same mistake the two youngsters did before them.

We pulled the beat-up van in the complex and made our way towards the back to where "Low" was ducked off. It was Gunz's idea to kidnap the nigga, so I let him come up with a way to get the nigga to the van. The last thing I wanted was to be seen in the same complex the nigga disappeared from.

"You sure this shit gonna work?" I asked Gunz.

"One thing these clowns can't resist is a gun. You show a nigga some shit he ain't got, you'll see the shit he'll do to get it." Gunz lifted the MP5s and Mini 14s.

We watched as a couple of guys looked towards the other, and I smiled when seeing Low push himself from the car and then limp towards us. This shit was just that easy.

***

Raylon

The minute I pulled into the drive and saw that Shoney's car was gone, I breathed a sigh of relief. I still hadn't called her back from earlier, and I was in need of a shower. I'd bathed at the hotel with Cindy, but I needed to rid myself of the fragrance she put on me afterwards. At first, I didn't think nothing of it, but when looking at the way she continually sprayed her perfume around me, and insisted on hugs after she'd freshened up, I kind of felt it was being done on purpose. I'd been dealing with hoes long enough to know the games they played, and I'd been with Shoney long enough to know the ways in which they did.

I also needed a few minutes to do a count myself. It had been a minute since I last did a count on the money I had at the house, and now that things had seemed to slow on Daxx's end, I was having to dig into my personal stash to get things done. I didn't know what he had going on with them dope heads he'd been running with, but I hoped they were not pressuring him into doing some shit he shouldn't have.

After a quick shower, I threw on a pair of boxers and ran the rest of my clothes down to the laundry room and mixed them in with the clothes Shoney was readying to be washed. This was the shit I had to do, because once she started sorting through clothes, it would be as if mine being mixed with hers caused them to smell a certain type of way.

The shit had been working for the longest, and I wasn't about to change now. I thought about looking into the fridge to see what I could make my wife for dinner but remembered that I had to make plans for the next drop. Once back in the room, I slid into some shorts, scented myself with Polo Sport, and opened my safe. It's about time Daxx dropped off, and that's the reason I called his ass.

***

Shoney

When seeing my husband's truck parked when I pulled up in the driveway, it surprised the hell out of me and pissed me off at the same time. I looked down at the watch he'd given me just days ago and noticed that he was earlier than he should have been. I prayed he hadn't discovered the surprise I had for him, because I was really debating whether to send the shit back and get my money—something Sept would have done. I intentionally left the cologne on the counter for when he arrived, but I wanted to be there to see the look on his face once I told him who it came from.

I'd learned years ago that Raylon wasn't the type of nigga you gave time to think. I'd learned that when it was something he didn't want to talk about or something he was caught lying about, the first thing he did was try to pull his dick out and fuck the shit out a bitch. That trick had even worked to my advantage many times. I walked in through the doors of my sitting area, listened for any signs that he was downstairs, and made my way into the kitchen. The bottle of Christian Dior was still sitting where I'd placed it, and nothing else seemed to be out of place.

I then walked back towards his theater room. Nothing there indicated that he'd been here. I headed up the stairs. My mind flashed a thought of him having a bitch in my bed, and that was one I really had to shake, because I would have been sitting in someone's county jail awaiting arraignment again, and I wasn't just saying the shit.

"Raylon," I called out once I was midway up the stairs.

If a bitch was up there, she'd better know how to scale a wall, because he'd have no choice but to push the bitch out of the window.

"I'm in the room, babe."

Before I even threw my bag onto the chair adjacent our bed, I froze. Raylon was kneeling, and in front of his face was a large amount of bills covering the bedroom floor.

"Dammit," I mumbled under my breath.

Raylon glanced in my direction and smiled. That's when I saw that he was on the phone, and that's when I took a deep breath. I nodded and headed for my walk-in closet.

"Let me get back at you," he told whoever was on the other end. "Where you coming from, babe?"

Some shit Sept once said came to mind, but instead of telling him that I'd just came from getting my pussy ate, I only said, "Fucking with that girl. She and another co-worker of ours got into it today."

"Yep, that sounds like her."

Raylon had stacks and stacks of bills aligned side by side, and if I was to guess the estimate, the amount I was looking at was just as much as Sept had shown me just minutes ago.

"Where are you taking all of that?" I asked, hoping to gauge where he was, as well as what he was doing.

"Just doing a count. It's been a minute."

I stepped out of my closet wearing only a peach-colored panty and bra set. "So how much are we looking at?" I asked in my attempt to disguise what I shouldn't have known.

Sept had kept a pretty good estimate of his money because of the shit she had going on. Therefore, I knew personally he was sitting on or around a quarter of a mill, if that.

"Well, if the damn horse pulls it off this weekend, we're going to be a hell of a lot richer," he told me before turning and acknowledging me and what I was wearing. "Where you finna go?"

"Nowhere. I'm just sliding into something comfortable," I told him before turning to give him a shot of the ass.

I knew my panties were wedged in the crack of my ass, and that had always driven him crazy. Just as I thought he was about to stand and head in my direction, he turned back to his money and scratched his head.

"Babe, have you been in the safe?"

I walked over to where he kneeled and began massaging his shoulders. I told him, "Not since the last time you had me go in there to get you some money and take it to that gambling shack." I rubbed his bald head and leaned down to kiss it. I told him, "I have a surprise for you."

"I must have did the shit the last time I—"

"Did what?" I asked, hoping that Sept hadn't taken more than she should have.

"The second row I had all of the stacks bottom side up, but this stack here was stacked right side up."

I closed my eyes because I'd asked her if she'd put everything back the way it was, and she assured me that she had. The last thing I needed was for Raylon to feel as if I'd been taking anything from him.

"So how much is missing?"

"Oh, nothing's missing. The money is good. It's just that I thought I had the stacks a certain way. It helps me when I do counts. When a stack is faced down, it's been here for a while, and when it's faced up, that means I'd recently added to what was already here."

While Raylon explained what Sept and I hadn't known, I knew I wasn't going to be letting her fuck up again. But to know that nothing was missing, it confirmed that she really did know what she was doing. I was walking past him when he spanked my ass and stood.

This was as good of a time as any, and when I did turn to him, I said, "A woman named Cindy West sent you a package today."

There was no pause in his movement and no other sign indicating that he even knew who she was, but his actions afterwards told me more than he ever would have. Raylon grabbed the rim of my panties and pulled me to him. He kissed me from my ear to my neck and to my breasts. I closed my eyes.

"What was it?" he mumbled around my titties. Raylon then reached for the clasp of my bra.

"A bottle of cologne," I told him before stepping back and looking him in his eyes.

"Them motherfuckers just trying to get another account."

"For what, Raylon?"

"You remember when I was telling you that I no longer wanted that woman Brent was fucking with to deal with my money?"

I nodded. I did remember hearing something about the chick Brent was using to clean the money he was playing with, but that was a conversation September and I had—I was sure.

"I guess she went and told one of her colleagues that I was up for grabs. They knew a nigga was flipping a few dollars, and I guess they felt as if they could make a little something also."

"Well, the cheap bitch couldn't even send the entire gift set. That alone should tell you what kind of shit they got going on," I told him.

The question of how she got my address was now answered, but still. It was something he wasn't telling me.

"I'm thinking about hiring her, though. The reports I've been getting from other guys I know are better than the ones we got about Sheila."

"Come downstairs. I want to show you something." I led Raylon into the kitchen, handed him the bottle of cologne, and pulled him towards the theater room. "You don't wear that shit no way."

The minute Raylon walked into the theater room, he smiled, and a thought came to mind. "You've been a good boy lately, so this is what good boys get."

"Bae, how much did all this cost?"

While Raylon walked from one item to the other, I stood and watched him. "I had to suck the manager's dick and give the delivery guys some pussy."

"Oh, really?" Raylon came towards me—his eyes on the camel toe between my legs. He scooped me up in one swift motion and sat me on the arm of one of the leather recliners. "Is that right?"

I laughed when he pushed me backward and raised my legs. My man was so strong, and it seemed as if he handled me without effort. "Boy, stop!" I squealed.

Once my panties were tossed across the room and I was bent over the arm of the recliner he'd pushed me on, I watched him climb behind me. I spread my legs for him.

"Naw, keep 'em closed. Keep them motherfuckers closed."

While Raylon stroked me from the back, I placed both my arms under my face and closed my eyes. I thought about some of the things Sept had said earlier. I thought about the day when it was all over, and the day I walked away from it all. That was something I knew I couldn't do. Especially when feeling him inside of me.

I told him, "And I had to fuck the guy that had me sign for the package Cindy West sent." I giggled when feeling Raylon go deeper and harder, and to make sure he worked for the nut, I began bucking against him. He loved when I did that.

"Give me this ass, Shoney! Give it to me!"

If it was one thing I needed my husband to know, it was that he had everything at home. Everything he needed was right here.

Chapter Twelve

Brent

That weekend, I made sure that things were in order as far as the guys were concerned. I was really looking forward to getting the shit over with and moving on to the next chapter of my life. I'd gotten up early, called Raylon before he could hit the streets, and reminded Daxx before he got full of that shit. I needed everyone in their right minds, and once it was agreed that we'd all meet up at Raylon's, I made a couple of rounds to both the shop and the lot to let my workers know that I'd be in later. It was something that could have been done via text, but I was really needing to get my thoughts together before confronting the guys that had been making sure I was fed for the longest.

When pulling into Raylon's driveway, the first thing I noticed was that Daxx was yet to show. And the second thing was that Shoney's M6 was gone, which meant that if the shit got out of hand, I was on my own. This wouldn't have been the first time we exchanged different views, but this would be one of the times I stood on the decision I'd made.

While waiting for Daxx to show, Raylon and I toured his new theater room, swapped a few ideas, and made our way outside. It was there our conversation turned towards the matters I was ready to discuss.

"Where this nigga at?"

Daxx had called a minute ago talking about he was making the block, but still hadn't shown. I prayed like hell he wasn't shooting a ghost, because he knew how bad I wanted to have this meeting. I'd even told him about acquiring several more properties, and I told him that I would be able to fund it on my own, so he didn't have to worry about me trying to bleed their pockets. That wasn't the reason for the get together.

"He'll be here." I thought about the last time he'd pulled the stunt of not showing when I needed him and said, "He'd better be."

"Knowing him, he's somewhere up under some tramp."

"Naw, that nigga should be pulling up any minute." I looked towards the street, then back to Raylon. I told him, "It's time to step outside of the box, Ray. I'm sitting on right at $460,000, got two establishments up and running, and I ain't trying to go backwards."

"What? Daxx cashed in already?"

"Naw, that nigga ain't did shit yet. That's why I'm trying to get at y'all."

"Where am I at, anyway?" Raylon asked.

I'd personally kept a ledger of all the money he and Daxx put into the businesses, just as I'd kept account of all the money they'd come to get from me. Yeah, they helped me make the shit happen, but this was where we were at the moment. "You've got about sixty-something grand invested."

"Sixty grand? Motherfucker, I've got more than that in the can alone."

Instead of a round with Raylon, I pulled out my phone and showed him damn near all of the electronic transactions, as well as all of the signatures of his when it was money he wanted me to give him to fund his bad gambling habits, as well as his personal affairs. It even surprised me to actually see how much he'd been blowing. This was one of the things Sheila had me to put into play, because she'd seen firsthand how people got lines crossed because they assumed.

"Nigga, I ain't got no $50,000 from you. You got that shit wrong."

"There you go with that shit, nigga." I pointed to the name under each. "You the only motherfucker I have dealings with named Raylon, and you the only motherfucker I'd even think about giving some money to." I stood and watched Raylon act as if his memory just wasn't serving him right.

"Damn."

"Yeah, damn. But I know you sitting on a bit, so that shit ain't hurting you," I told him.

I knew about the shipments he had coming from Reynosa, and I also knew he wasn't paying as much for them as he had in the beginning.

"Motherfucker, I've been having to spend just as much as I make." Raylon pointed behind us. "This house, these cars and trucks, my work. Shoney's broke ass, and—"

I cut him off by adding, "Your gambling debts."

"Yeah, that too. I've got bills now."

"Daxx told me y'all was making around $8000 a month on the spots alone."

"Yeah, that was before this nigga started fucking with them niggas he been riding with."

"What you sitting on, anyway?"

"I'm right at half a mill, if not more."

I knew when Raylon was lying his ass off, and for me to see the familiar demeanor, I looked at him with a raised brow and asked, "You broke, nigga?"

"Hell naw, I ain't broke. I'm good. Me and Shoney good."

"Then it's time we do something else with what we got, Raylon. This street shit ain't going to last too much longer, homie."

"Aw, there you go with that janky ass shit."

"Naw, that's real. And besides, we all agreed to put this shit behind us sooner than later. We've been lucky, Ray, and you know it. We've had to scratch our way from the bottom and—"

"Motherfucker, you ain't scratched shit but your ass. While you were sitting up in that damn barbershop cleaning clippers, me and Daxx was out here in these streets cleaning house. You ain't put in no work, nigga."

I regarded Ray as if he was a mime. The work I put in might not have been behind a pistol, but he needed to be reminded of the shit I did and have been doing. I told him, "Yeah, that's only because we didn't need motherfuckers looking at me when seeing the shit you and that nigga, Daxx, was doing. I'm the motherfucker leaning off the helm of the ship with my arms wide open. I'm the motherfucker the cops, feds, and IRS are going to come fucking with if this shit falls apart. And then, there's no telling what will happen to Sheila, because her name is just as visible as mine when it comes to looking at all the shit we've made happen."

"You know what I'm talkin' about, fat ass nigga."

No sooner did I remind Ray of my role in the shit we had going on, an all-black S-Class Benz pulled into the driveway. I strained to see who was behind the wheel of the customized luxury car. "You expecting company?" I asked.

"Not at all."

The customizations on the car alone most likely had cost just as much as the car, and because I had all kinds of requests for certain kits and modifications, I was able to factor that without being told. I shook my head when the driver's side door opened and Daxx climbed out. I knew the nigga was needing some wore wheels, but damn.

"What's good, Ray. Big Boy?"

"What the fuck is that, Daxx?" I asked and nodded towards the car. I watched Daxx smile.

"That's a 2019 S-63 with the Brabus kit." Daxx turned back towards the car and said, "$114,000."

When Raylon took a step towards the car, I did also. But we were on two entirely different trains of thought. Raylon leaned forward, squinted, and asked, "Who the fuck in the car?"

"Oh, that's Rubberhead and Gunz," Daxx replied as if it was nothing.

"You bring these niggas to my house, Daxx? What the fuck is wrong with you, man?"

"Them niggas ain't studying you, Ray. We got some shit lined up, and I need them to be in pocket."

I jumped in the conversation. "You spent a hundred grand on that, Daxx?"

"The hundred wasn't shit. That don't even hurt me. Hell, it's about time a nigga rewarded himself for the shit I accomplished."

"I can't believe you brought these motherfucking dope heads to my house, nigga."

"These the same niggas that's making trips for you, nigga. It's because of these niggas you're able to live the way you are. Don't forget about that."

"Motherfucker, business is business, but the shit you doing making it personal. I'll bet not one of them niggas you got working know where you lay your head. This ain't some spot, nigga. This is where me and my wife sleep at night."

"Um, don't you think that's a little too much for a nigga that's said to be employed at a detail shop, Daxx?" I asked him, knowing where things were going between him and Ray.

"I know how to buy a fucking car, nigga."

"Does Sheila know about this?"

"What the fuck that bitch got to know about the way I spend my money? Fuck that bitch."

"And what's up with the money you were supposed to be picking up?" Ray asked.

"I ain't got to the shit yet."

I stood and listened to the exchange between Daxx and Raylon and knew I wasn't going to be able to address what needed to be addressed. And once they started arguing over money owed, I knew it was just a matter of time before this entire meeting was over.

"What the fuck you mean by that?" Raylon asked when hearing that a couple of the spots were closed.

"I'm doing what I got to do out here. You ain't even got time to make the rounds, but you screaming about how I'm going about it."

"Motherfucker, don't forget this is just as much my shit as it is yours."

"Ray, you ain't even got no runners to traffic your shit. I got the niggas I fuck with taking chances for you, and you don't even want to pay them. I've got workers peeling a nigga for money, and when I tell you about it, you ain't tripping, but at the end of the same sentence, you want your cut. How in the fuck you mean 'how does it work?'"

"Nigga, you the one calling us talking about you got hit and you had to do this and that and take a loss here and there, but you turn around and pull up in a $100,000 car. What the fuck you mean?"

"Hold up, y'all. We getting all the way off track," I told them, seeing what had been seen many times before.

"Hold up, my ass, Brent. And your pussy-whipped ass talking about giving that bitch, Sept, $100,000, but you want us to put money behind the shit you—"

I raised my hand instead of allowing Daxx to continue. I told him. "That was my personal money. The money I gave her didn't have shit to do with what we got going on."

"Yeah, that's what you say. Them shops ain't pulling in that much money."

I reached for my phone, but instead of showing him account numbers and some of the other shit Sheila and I were able to put together, I just said. "Have you forgotten about the business loans I got and didn't need so we could get this shit started?"

"I'm talking about the other numbers right now," Ray said.

"Matter of fact, don't you owe me $50,000 for the buy-ins on them horses?" Daxx crossed his arms while awaiting his answer.

"Yeah, I still owe that, but we agreed that it would be paid after the races. And they race later today." Raylon looked down at his watch, then back to Daxx, who was still standing with his arms folded.

"Well, let's take care of that before we start talking about other issues. If you were handling your business instead of running behind these hoes, you'd know where the money was," Daxx told him before heading back to his car.

"Nigga, we ain't finished!" I yelled after him.

"I am."

"You gonna end up just like them niggas, Daxx!"

Daxx got to the driver's side door, turned around, and told Ray, "I'm rich because of these niggas. Not y'all."

That was what caused me to raise my hand and give Daxx the middle finger. It was also the statement that made me realize what I had to do. I turned to Raylon and told him, "I'm going to get with Sheila and have the rest of that money sent to you. I'm through with this shit, homie." I threw up my hands. "I'm through."

Chapter Thirteen

Shoney

The weekend had come and gone. For most of it, I was trying to figure out just what Sept was doing. Although she'd shown me money and Raylon spoke of none missing from his stash, I was still scratching my head when it came to the shit my girl was doing. And with Brent giving her $100,000 to go along with what she had herself, I was trying to get her to do something with it. I knew what I wanted to do, but I also knew it couldn't be done anytime soon.

We both came to work today hoping for the best and expecting the worst, and quiet as kept, I knew Sept was a nervous wreck. The anticipation had me looking from my computer to the window, and from the window to Mr. Dillan's office. So I knew she was tripping, even though she wasn't showing it.

"That bitch, Alyssa, called in this morning," Sept told me when she walked up to my cubicle.

"Yeah, I know. That bitch gonna file all kinds of medical leaves and shit. I wouldn't be surprised if the bitch didn't have to come to work for another year," I told her.

"Mr. Dillan said the bitch had to go to the ER to get some of the staples removed. He said if the cops do come asking him anything, he's going to say he didn't see shit."

I tsked and asked, "And you believe him?"

"That motherfucker had better not say shit."

"Do you think they're going to come here looking for you? I mean, the bitch do know where you work, if nothing else."

"Well, if the bitch do, we both going to jail because she hit me first." Sept shrugged and continued. "I got bond money, so I'm good. I'll be out in a couple of hours, and Brent is already on top of the lawyer, so fuck it."

I closed my eyes and shook my head. I remembered vividly how I had to go through the process. The book-in, the arraignment, getting assigned housing, and the "shitter critters." I remembered all of that shit. "Ughh! I hated that shit."

"I'm going to have that bitch fucked off if she did go snitch a bitch out," Sept whispered.

"Whatever the case, though, I got you, Sept. You know I got you," I told her before standing to hug her. She'd been there for me from day one, and I was going to be there with her until the last. I promised.

***

I pointed.

"What?"

"You see how many people in that gym over there? People are serious about their health these days, Sept. I'm really wanting to open me one." We were out on our lunch break and decided to go grab some smoothies.

"I thought we were talking about that nigga you calling husband."

I pulled her along. "For the most part, he's been doing good by me."

"What that nigga say about the lipstick then?"

"I forgot to even ask, Sept. I really did."

"I bet you didn't forget to give him the pussy. I'm beginning to think you got a fetish for the shit, Shoney."

"Shut up, Sept." I led her towards a bench seating and sat down.

"I'm serious, Shoney. Some women be on shit like that. They blame their husbands for some shit, knowing they'd get spoiled for a few days, fucked down, and treated like queens. Then it's back to the same shit again. You might need to seek some counseling, because it sounds like you crazy."

"And you need to seek some counseling, because your fetish is scheming, plotting, and some of everything else when it comes to money."

"I know these niggas out here ain't loyal. That's why I get it how I live. I'll be damn if I be one of them bitches that chase a nigga just so he'll love me. Next thing you know, he'll be like, *'You got to suck my homebody dick and let him fuck too, if you want to be with me.'* And you have some of these dirty ass hoes that do the shit. Like you."

"Whatever, Sept. You know I ain't doing no shit like that for nobody." I only shook my head and rolled my eyes because she knew me better than that, but the woman was known for saying anything.

"You've got to tax they ass, Shoney. I used to rip when I heard about a bitch setting a nigga up and having him robbed, but now, I understand the shit. Now, I be like, they should have killed his ass too."

"Oh, and he asked me if I'd been in his safe." It wasn't too long ago that I'd met a chick that felt the same way. Hell, she was living that life. I looked over at my girl in thought. She'd become that same way before long.

"You should have told his punk ass yeah."

While sitting there listening to Sept go on and on about the way niggas treated women and the way women allowed them, my thoughts went to the woman named Cyclone. She might not have come out and said the shit, but she knew exactly who Raylon was and what he was about. He might have been known to lose a few dollars, but he didn't fuck over women like men did, and for that, I was grateful.

"You hear me, Shoney?"

"Huh, what you say?" I smiled.

"You sitting here thinking about some dick, ain't you? You are sad, Shoney. Real sad."

"No, I'm not thinking about no dick," I told her and had to laugh, because I hadn't gotten to that part yet.

***

Raylon

For it to have been the beginning of the week, the Shack was packed, and the thrill of the win was heavy in the air. I made sure I checked in with the house, got me a line of credit, and stalked the tables for any that would be a lick. I'd lost a couple of dollars over the weekend, but it was nothing I couldn't get back. Before entertaining the guys around the dice or poker tables, I tried calling Daxx several times. I needed to get at him about some business I needed taken care of.

"What's up, Ray?"

"Nigga, I've been calling you all morning. Where you at?"

"Been busy, nigga. You know how this shit goes."

From the tone of Daxx's voice, I could tell that he'd either been up all night, or was fucking with that shit, but instead of going off on him for that, I got right to the point. "I need some help, Daxx. I lost over $100,000 fucking with them niggas in Oklahoma, and I'm trying to get it back."

"So, what do you want me to do about it?"

"Slide me a couple of dollars until I get right," I told him.

"I've got my shit tied up right now, but I can throw you about $1,500."

"Fifteen hundred? What the fuck is that going to do, nigga?" I couldn't believe this nigga was trying to play me with some shit like that. He knew I was good for the shit.

"That's all I got right now. Take it or leave it, nigga."

I nodded my understanding. He was still tripping on that bullshit from the other day. I told him, "I'll tell you what, nigga. You take that shit and stick it up your ass. And from now on, I'll be picking up my own money."

"Sounds good to me, hustler."

I ended the call with Daxx, looked around the room of the gambling shack, and phoned Brent. I knew that nigga had some cash to play with. Hell, if it wasn't for me, his ass wouldn't have had that.

***

Brent

Halfway to the shop, my phone rang. I was expecting to hear from Daxx or either Raylon because I still had some choice words for the both of them, but when seeing Sheila's contact info, I exhaled, let off a little steam, and picked up. "Hey, you. What's up?"

"That's what I need to be asking you. How'd it go with the guys?"

"To hell. They got to tripping, shit spiraled out of control fast, and before you knew it, Daxx charged Raylon up about some money and—"

"So you didn't tell either of them that you were stepping away from the illegal activities?"

"Well, I threw it at Daxx when he was leaving, and I did tell Raylon." I pulled into the shop, parked, and climbed out.

"And what did he have to say about that?"

"You know how niggas is. He started asking about the money he had tied up in the business, and I even had to show him. Oh, yeah. I did tell him that I would have you transfer the funds whenever he wanted them."

"Um, okay. Just have him contact me with the details. I'll Take care of that ASAP."

"I sure do appreciate it, Sheila. The sooner I get these niggas out of my pockets, the sooner I'll be able to breathe and think."

I talked to Sheila for a few more minutes before hanging up. So much had been going on that I'd forgotten all about the shit I told Sept I'd do. Fucking with everybody else had me forgetting about my own girl. But then, my phone rang again.

"What's up, Raylon? How'd it go for you?" I asked, hoping that this was the call made where he'd either came around to accepting what I was about to do, or wanting to do the right thing by leaving all the other bullshit alone and focusing on getting this money.

I'd tried getting at Daxx, but he'd been in the streets for the past couple of days, and when I did call, he sent my shit to voicemail.

"Where you at?"

"Right now, I'm at the lot. What's up?"

"Say, Brent. I need a few dollars until I bounce back."

"What you mean, a few dollars?" I thought of him trying to contact Daxx and asked, "Have you heard form Daxx since Saturday?"

"Fuck that nigga, Brent. He's going to need a nigga before long, and I'm going to smile, pat him on the back, and tell him not to worry about it, and that it's going to be okay."

"What y'all trippin' on now?"

"Nigga, I need about $100k. I lost a few dollars at the track and need to get back on. The money we got tied up in the spots is on hold because Daxx on some more shit, and I had to go ahead and pay the front of the drop."

I sighed, closed my eyes, and dropped my head. I was not about to go there with Raylon. I was not about tie myself in with what he had going on. Let alone give him $100,000. "I wish you would have gotten at me before now, man. I had to give Sept $100,000 for the shit she's trying to do."

"Man, don't bullshit me, Brent. I'm going to give the shit right back, nigga. Damn."

"Nigga, didn't you just tell me two days ago that you were sitting on a half a mill? Spend the shit. I'm not going to give you my shit when you sitting on just as much as I got."

I knew the nigga was lying the other day, but this only confirmed the shit I already knew.

"I'm smoked out. This shit come and go, nigga! And you know I know how to go and get this shit, Brent."

I wanted to tell him that he also knew how to lose it but chose not to. I only told him, "I spoke with Sheila earlier, and she told me to tell you call her, and she was going to send that $60,000 wherever you want it sent."

"Oh, yeah, yeah. That's right. Um, what's her number again?"

As soon as I hung up with Raylon, Shoney's picture popped up on my phone, and my heart began double-timing. I knew something was wrong.

"Hey, Shoney. What's up?"

"They came and picked her up, Brent. Not too long after we got back from our lunch break. She told me to call you."

I could tell that Shoney had been crying, and to comfort her as best I could, I told her, "I'm on it right now. She'll be out as soon as I can get here."

"Don't leave that girl hanging, Brent. If you ain't got it done in the next hour, I'm going to get Raylon to get her."

My telling Shoney that Raylon had just called me begging for money was something I couldn't do. Besides, I didn't have to, because I wasn't going to do anything else. "I'm walking out of the shop now."

"I'll tell you what. You just post the bail, and I'll pick her up."

"Sounds like a plan," I told her before ending the call and dialing a number of the bail bondsman I knew. The one I'd sold an SUV for his daughter's graduation.

***

Daxx

"You see all the shit that nigga got in the driveway?" I asked Rubber and Gunz once we'd left Raylon's home.

I wasn't tripping about giving him the money for the buy-in, because it should have been something he gave back without complaint, but for him to charge me up about the money I was out here making sure we got, I wasn't feeling that shit. He might have come down on Brent that way, but I was just as much of a boss as he was.

"And he tripping on giving up a punk ass $5,000?" Gunz added.

"Roach ass nigga might need to be stepped on a couple of times," said Rubber.

I half laughed, thinking of just that. But instead of entertaining the idea, I told them, "He's good at fucking it off himself. I'll bet you that nigga lose that house within the next couple of years. Paid for or not."

"That nigga must not realize that his contacts see my face more than him. I just might need to start scoring and getting credit from the same motherfuckers and leaving him with the bill. See, he ain't thought about no shit like that," Rubber went on.

I had been thinking about the same things for a while and knew that if Raylon did get caught up and called himself hanging me out of the window, I was going to do exactly that. Only thing was, I didn't know his contacts like that, but now that I'd been feeding the very motherfuckers that did, it was a thought to revisit later.

***

Raylon

The day I'd been waiting for had finally arrived. So much shit had been going on that I was neglecting what really mattered at the time, and that was where I was putting the lion's share of my money. I'd already gotten with a few guys that had made their fortune betting on the races and was pretty sure I had a decent pick. I wasn't even trying to select a winner of the Derby. All I needed was for the horses I chose to place within the top five. I'd already put the $50,000 needed for the buy-in in place, but I was needing more.

Now that Daxx was tripping with the shit we had going on, and Brent—with his scary ass—was listening to some woman about how she felt our business should be conducted, and the way our money should be spent, I had to make the better moves for myself and Shoney. It wasn't like Shoney had a hustle going on and I could sit back and cross my legs. I was the one that had to make this shit pay off.

I'd been talking with a few of the guys from OKC in the parking lot earlier, and by the way they were rolling, I knew they had money to blow, and that's why I upped the ante when it came to putting money where my mouth was.

"Let's make this shit interesting," I told the guy that had climbed out of the gold Bentley Flying Spur. He was said to have been the owner of some luxury car lot, and being that I was damn near in the same line of work, I saw it as a play that could have been beneficial to me and Brent.

"I'll play you a little over $100,000," he came back, really trying to run up the bar and run off the niggas that wasn't talking about shit.

I thought for a few seconds, reached in my glove compartment for the title to Shoney's M6, and told him, "Here's the title to a fairly new BMW M6 I just acquired a couple of weeks ago. If you can match that, you got yourself a bet." I was no stranger to the ego play, and that's why I added, "It shouldn't be shit for someone like you."

"And how do I know that car isn't sitting in some shop totaled or something?"

"That sounds like some shit a motherfucker would say when they pockets ain't as big as they mouth." I began folding the title.

"I'll tell you what, city slicker. I got a Mulsanne I just put on the lot, and I'll put that up against that BMW. How about that?"

Once we shook and handed the titles to the guy we both knew, we walked into the entrance of the derby. The smile I wore was because I was back on my shit, and even if I did lose, it wasn't coming out of my pockets. I could always get Shoney another car. That wasn't shit now that we had the car lot and access to the police auctions.

***

Shoney

After taking care of things for September and waiting for Brent's guys to come and get her car, I prepared to leave myself. I heard some of the things being said around the office, and unlike Sept, I found some of them amusing. Someone had said something about she got picked up because she got caught boosting high-end clothes from the Galleria, and someone else said that she'd had Alyssa kidnapped because of the fight they had Friday, and her absence only fueled that. When it came to the people that thought they knew Sept, I started to make one of my own just to be doing it, but my girl had other shit I needed to be worrying about.

Once it was understood that I'd stop by the house, get out of my work clothes, and grab a bite to eat, I was going to the county jail so I could be there when she walked out. I grabbed my shit and made my way out. It shocked the hell out of me when Mr. Dillan called me into his office and said, *"I'll even appear at her hearing and tell them how much of a good person September is."*

I'd called Raylon a couple of times, just in case Brent didn't come through on his end, but only got his voicemail. I left a message telling him to get back at me ASAP, because this was some important shit. I couldn't help but be reminded of my stay in jail and knew personally that if Sept did have to dress out and go upstairs, she was going to have a fight. As pretty as she was, they were sure to size her up, and as stupid as she was, she wasn't about to do anything other than that.

I frowned when pulling into my driveway, because the drivers had to have come to the wrong address. I climbed out, saw the two guys walking towards me, and waited.

"Mrs. Edwards?"

"That would be me," I told the tall white guy. I looked over at the guy and smiled.

"Um, we've come to pick up the car you're driving."

I shook my head and told them, "No, they already picked up the car that was supposed to be picked up." I watched as he flipped the page on the clipboard, walked around to confirm my license plate number, and frowned.

"Are you married to Raylon Edwards?"

"Yes, I am."

"Well, it says here that this car was purchased by my boss two days ago."

"Excuse me?" I snatched the clipboard from his hand and turned it to where I could see signatures, and sure as shit got pushed out of an ass, Raylon's signature was signed above another signature on the title of the car he'd bought for me. "He sold my car?" I asked them, really not needing to hear either of them say the shit again.

"The way I was told, the car was lost at the track. I didn't know we'd be traveling all the way to Dallas to get it."

"Where are you guys from?" I asked before pulling out my phone and dialing Raylon's number for the umpteenth time.

"Oklahoma."

It was then that I noticed the huge Oak City Motors sign painted on the doors of the flat-bed wrecker. I couldn't believe this shit, but it didn't surprise me one bit. "That's why his punk ass ain't picking up his phone," I told them before handing them the key fob.

I could have stood there and asked if a mistake was made, but I had other things to do. I guess me knowing I had money of my own now caused me to overlook the small shit. Either that, or I'd been through the shit so much I was numb to it.

Chapter Fourteen

September

Me having to depend and wait on Brent was really the only thing I had to shake, because I'd been in jail before, and I knew about the process. And now that I was here, I could do nothing else but wait. Once I was placed in the holdover with about thirty other women, I made my way past the phones and the line leading up to them. I hated giving up my watch, because the way they were eyeing my shit, there was no telling if it would make it into the property room. I stepped over a couple of sleeping figures and couldn't believe how tired I was myself. It was always places that wouldn't allow you to do shit else, that you actually realized all the things you had to do.

I sat as far as I could from the toilet because bitches were some of the nastiest motherfuckers on the planet, and being locked up with a bunch of ovulating and cycle-having hoes with no proper way to care for themselves had a bitch wishing she did have a dick. The entire holdover smelled like ass and piss, and I was more than sure that by the time I walked out, I would be in need of a scented oil bath, some new clothes, and a walk through of some perfume mist.

"Hey. September, right?"

I looked up when I noticed the woman from that day when Shoney stopped me from kicking her ass while I was at work. I gave her a sideways look and said, "Yeah, what's up?"

"I thought that was you when you came in. What they got you in for?"

I had no choice but to slide over a bit when seeing her look as if she was wanting to squeeze in between me and the heavyset woman I'd sat beside.

"Kicking a bitch's ass," I told her loud enough for the other motherfuckers in attendance to hear also.

"That sounds about right. Shoney did tell me that you were off the field risk. Speaking of Shoney. How's she doing?"

I wanted to be mad and let her know I didn't feel like doing any talking, but I had to hear more about the conversation she and Shoney had. Besides, she really sounded as if she had a few things to get off her chest.

"She's good. But what's up with you?" I asked.

It was apparent by her attire that she was still being dragged by the same niggas we talked about that day in my cubicle. I watched her exhale, lower her head, and smile.

"I should have listened to you, September. I really should have. The nigga I'm with got a dope case, and he needed me to take it so he wouldn't go to jail. He told me that he was going to get me a good lawyer, and I'd only get probation."

I closed my eyes. The rest of the story didn't even have to be told, but since she was talking, I let her fill me in.

"I should have been made bail by now, but he said he has to collect some money from some of the guys he hustles with."

"If he's got to do that for bond money, how in the hell is he going to get you a lawyer?"

"That's what I'm sitting here thinking about now," she said with her eyes downcast.

"Stop being that bitch…" I caught myself before going off on her. I'd forgotten her name, so I asked. "Stop being that stupid bitch, Reniya. As long as you allow niggas to drag you, that's exactly what they're going to do. You dun took a charge for a nigga, and he ain't even got the means to come bail you out. How much is it, anyway?'

"$50,000. All he got to pay is ten—"

"Yeah, I know what the nigga got to pay, but that should be something you can pay yourself." I looked from her to a couple of the other young girls that were listening. It wasn't hard to notice that they were young, pretty, and caught up from some shit they really didn't have anything to do with. "When you bitches start seeing y'all potential, them niggas will also, but 'til then, y'all gonna be in and out of here like Walmart."

"I thought the nigga loved me," one girl said from the back of the room. She was chocolate like my girl but on the slim side. But instead of changing diapers with them, I said, "Y'all forming habits for these niggas, and they ain't benefiting y'all at all. Change the way you treat yourselves first, then demand the shit from whoever else." I sat and gave them bitches game until Reniya's name was called.

Instead of making bail, she was headed upstairs like a few more of the girls that were depending on niggas to do for them. It was then I came up with a plan, 'cause if they let a nigga drag them for nothing, I was going to see just how far they'd go to make something happen for themselves.

"I'll tell y'all what," I told her and the chocolate chick that reminded me so much of my girl. "Give me y'all information, and if them niggas ain't did nothing by the time I step out, I'm going to post it."

"Don't bullshit me, September, because I need to be out there with my kids."

I hurried to hand them both some tissue so they could scribble their names and dates of birth. This would be me giving back, as well as a part of the plan Shoney and I had been putting into play for a minute.

"And what am I going to owe you?" asked the chocolate chick.

I smiled and told her, "Your soul." I looked down at the piece of tissue she handed me while walking them towards the door. "Coffee?"

"Yep. Momma spilled an entire cup when she found out she was pregnant, so that's how she got burned twice. Me and a cup of coffee."

Before either of us could get in a good laugh, the far door opened, and my name was called. It was time for me to see what they had me charged with.

"Good luck, September."

I waved at Reniya, winked at Coffee, and followed the guard out. I didn't care what my bond was. Brent had better have his ass out there ready.

Chapter Fifteen

Shoney

Frank Crowley Courthouse

By the way people pointed and stared at us, you would have sworn I was the one appearing for the evidentiary hearing, and Sept was some high-paid attorney. When I say the woman went overboard? I mean, all the way over. The woman was dressed like she'd just stepped off the pages of *Esquire Magazine*. The executive suit, the Versace heels, oversized Prada shades, and the Louis Vuitton briefcase she carried screamed high profile, and as bad as I wanted this hearing to sail under the radar, it wasn't about to happen. Several people had already asked which court were we going to, and I was sure one of them was a reporter for one of the more prominent news outlets swarming around the courthouse.

The minute we stepped off of the elevator, Sept's attorney waved us over wearing an expression that should have raised red flags and had us running for the nearest exit. But I was here with my girl, and if she was sure of the play she had in motion, then I was going to go along with it.

"Ms. Hassan, I was beginning to think you weren't going to show," he told her before walking us over to where we could talk in private.

I couldn't help but stare at the lawyer, because I was sure I'd seen him on television before. He was an older white guy with salt and pepper, stringy hair, and his beard was predominantly white and flawless, and all of the suit-clad men that passed by simply referred to him as Peter.

"Traffic." Sept removed her shades and handed them to me.

I rolled my eyes, placed them inside my purse, and looked towards the doors of the courtroom.

"Well, the alleged victim still hasn't shown up, and the judge is set to hear the case against you in ten minutes."

"Perfect."

I really didn't know what it all meant, and that was the reason I asked him. "And what happens to September if the other woman doesn't show?"

"Then the hearing could possibly be postponed, if the judge grants the request by the prosecution."

"Prosecution?" I asked before looking at Sept, who was a little bit more composed than she should have been.

"Will you please chill out, Shoney? We've got this."

"This is only a hearing of both parties. I'm well aware of the legalities, and I'm going to see if I can have the court move to dismiss if the victim doesn't show. I have a statement from you all's supervisor..." Peter then reached into his satchel, pulled out a couple of sheets of paper, and handed them to Sept, who then handed them to me—as if she knew the content of them. "...claiming that employee, Alyssa Patterson, both started the altercation and assaulted Ms. Hassan first. I also have the photos Ms. Hassan had taken by medical staff at Parkland Memorial."

I knew that was a damn lie, because I was the one that took those pics, and by the way they both were looking at me, it was understood that I was really the one being put in the loop.

"Are they offering her any kind of plea agreement?" The only reason I asked was because I'd heard the shit on *Law and Order* and still wanted him to know that I did have some type of legal acumen.

They both smiled.

"Shoney, just sit back and ride."

Once Peter stood and made his way into the courtroom, I turned to Sept and whispered, "And what if the bitch strolls up in here telling a different version of the story we all know, Sept?"

"Then that means them bitches ain't about shit, and we're back to the square root of it."

"What bitches? I'm hoping like hell you ain't depending on none of our co-workers to come to bat for you. Damn near all of them would like to see your ass in cuffs."

"You'll see."

When seeing a crowd of people exit the elevators and head in our direction, I immediately looked for Alyssa, because there was no way in hell she'd miss the opportunity to stick it to Sept. I glanced over at Sept, but she was more concerned about her phone than anything else. I exhaled once the crowd passed us by, and there was no Alyssa.

"Shoney, call ya husband or something, because you're about to piss me off."

I looked at my watch, saw that we had around six minutes before the hearing started, and shook my head. And after composing myself as best I could, I crossed one leg over the other and pulled out my phone. I hadn't written in my journal in a while. I needed to call Mr. Dillan and thank him, and I had a feeling I was about to lie when it came to my husband. "I sure hope you know what you're doing, Sept. I really do."

"If it will make you feel any better, the bitch ain't going to show, Shoney."

I looked from the courtroom door to Sept, saw her thumb out a text, and asked, "How can you be so sure?"

She handed me her phone and said, "Pretty Girl Power."

I gasped when seeing that it was actually Alyssa on the screen. It was apparent that she'd been crying her eyes out, and by the way her mouth was gagged and her hair disheveled, she was being held against her will. I regarded my girl without question, and she only winked and said, "Let's go in here and get this shit dismissed."

"Sept, did you—"

"Bring your ass on, Shoney. I told you, we got this."

***

Daxx

After retrieving the van from the spot Brent had it delivered, we all climbed in and made our way to where the OGs were said to have hung out. It was agreed that if we caught them all together, we'd carry out the hit. There was no need in hunting them down separately, and there was no leaving any of them alive. We were parked down the block from the hole-in-the-wall hangout.

"What we looking like?" I asked while putting on the all-black uniform I'd picked up from the thrift store the day before.

"So far, I've counted seven that went in and didn't come out."

"The more, the merrier," Rubber added before checking the magazine he was loading into the fully automatic assault rifle he held.

"And three of them are kids," Gunz continued, knowing the argument me and Raylon had about the subject.

"Fuck 'em," Rubberhead hissed before handing me the assault rifle with the bump stock.

"I hope these clowns got something up in there worth our while," I told them, being that they were said to have been plotting a hit on the three of us. I was at least hoping they had some artillery, if nothing else.

"I'm looking at the structure of the building, and I say we just run the back of this motherfucker through the front door. Then we murder their asses," Gunz advised.

I watched Rubberhead smile, nod his understanding, and look towards me. "You drive, Daxx. Let me and Gunz show these young ass niggas what war looks like." He climbed into the back of the partially empty van, pulled at the door handle, and continued. "Hit they ass like a smash and grab."

"It's too many to snatch, and we ain't going to be running around that motherfucker looking for nobody, so—"

"So we burn the bitch to the ground afterwards. Whoever is left can fade that fire the best way they know how," I told them before sliding on the ball cap and shades.

"You just make sure you back this motherfucker straight into the door. Me and Rubber gonna blast on they ass from the windows, so no one will get hurt on this end."

"Y'all ready?" I pulled away from the curb and made our way towards the hangout spot. It was once again showtime.

***

Raylon

Against my better judgement, I went ahead and followed Asia out to the Galleria. She'd begged me until the point to where I had no choice, and since I was leaving drugs at her house, there was no way I could say no. I'd already called to see where Shoney was, and after remembering that Sept's hearing was this morning, I knew I was in the clear and would make the stop with Asia. I was about to make a grip in the OKC, and knowing that I was not about to get back to Asia anytime soon, I went ahead and stuck my foot in my mouth and told her I'd buy whatever it was she liked.

I'd been shopping with Shoney a thousand times and pretty much knew there was nothing I couldn't afford, but once Asia pulled me inside of the small boutique and pointed to a handbag that cost an unbelievable $16,000, I shook my head. This was the same handbag I refused to buy Shoney. There was no way in hell I was going to spend that much money on something that would eventually end up on the floor of her closet, or stowed away on the shelf.

"Come on, Asia, you can't be serious."

"I need that bag, Raylon!" She beamed with excitement. "Please."

"There were only two shipped to this branch, and Kelly Rowland bought the first," the sales guy said, adding fuel to the fire Asia didn't need.

I knew the motherfucker was lying his ass off, because I'd heard the pitch from Shoney and September already, and when they told the story, Beyoncé was the one that bought the damn bag, and it was three that came instead of two. I eyed the faggot contemptuously before looking down at Asia.

She pointed to a pair of knee-high lace-up boots and said, "And I need them boots to go with it."

I didn't mind spending $1,800 for the boots, and when looking at them, I was sure Shoney didn't own a pair.

"When did those come in?" I asked while pointing at the same boots Asia took a liking to.

"Just got ordered two days ago," said the sales guy.

I smiled at him, 'cause a lie wasn't shit to tell, but he was hustling, and I had to respect the game. "I'll take one handbag and two pairs of those boots." I had to get my wife a pair.

"Thanks, babe." Asia gave me a kiss and winked at the guy that just made a nice commission off of three items. "You can go see that other bitch now."

I kissed Asia on the forehead, grabbed the bag I'd later give to my wife, and headed for the parking lot. Asia still had a couple grand to fuck off, and I had somewhere to be and money to make. But first, I had to have some of that pussy Cindy was sitting on.

***

Daxx

"Y'all ready?" I asked the two of them as we were about to pass the spot.

"Play the song, nigga."

On cue, I swung the van away from the spot and threw it in reverse. From where I sat, I could see that people really didn't know what the hell was going on, and once they did put shit together, it was too late. I smashed into the front doors of the hangout with the rear of the van, and true to his word, we barreled through wood, sheet rock, and burglar bars at the same time. Before I could come to a halt, Rubberhead and Gunz were already firing a series of shots into the place, and in such close quarters, the gunfire and screams were deafening.

I threw the van in park and leaned out of the driver's side window with the rifle I had. It barked fire and the bump stock absorbed the recoil perfectly. I fired at a couple of guys that looked to be going for either pistols or cover, and once one was knocked off of his feet, and the other unsuccessfully tried to shield himself with a screaming woman, I took aim at a couple more guys I didn't see at first.

Shots were fired in my direction, and I could feel shattered glass from the windshield bounce off the shades I was wearing. I ducked, raised the weapon above me, and squeezed the trigger while moving, aiming the rifle in a sweeping motion.

"They heated!" I yelled at Rubber and Gunz, who were firing continual shots out of the back of the van windows.

"The back, Daxx! They ran for the back!" Rubberhead screamed over the heavy blast of gunfire.

Just as I was about to open the door and head that way, I heard Gunz scream out in pain.

"Aghhh! Shit, I'm hit! I'm hit!"

"Gunz got hit, Daxx! Let's go! Let's go!" Rubber yelled.

I tried to slam the van in drive, but the gear was caught, so I threw it in reverse in a gear below. "Shit!" I yelled.

Gunz had said there were only seven people inside, but it was now that we realized there had to be more than that because of how much gun fire there was. There was a short pause in the gunfire before Rubber began firing off from a second clip. The van launched forward, throwing Rubber off balance. Several of his shots pierced the inside of the van, and the radio in front of me exploded. I straightened the van as best I could when hitting the street, and once Rubber found his balance, he began firing at the guys that seemed to have come from the rear of the building. I hit the steering wheel with both hands.

"God dammit, Gunz!" Not only did the hit go sideways, but now Gunz was hit. "You alright?"

"They got him in the neck and shoulder," Rubber said once we were a way off from the scene.

"I'm taking him to Methodist!"

With the windshield shot to shit and bullet holes painting the majority of the van, I flew down Hampton.

"We've got company, Daxx!"

I was expecting to see a car load of niggas, but instead, I was looking at the red and blue lights of two patrol cars behind us, and before I could make the light and possibly shake the cops, Rubberhead began firing at the cars that chased us.

"Drive this motherfucker, Daxx!"

I tried to look back to see what Gunz's condition was like, but was blindsided by another van that had the right of way. I fought with the steering wheel as best I could, tried to get us out of the spin the other van caused, and felt the van jump the curb. I saw the pile seconds before we collided into it, and as slow as things were happening, I couldn't control anything. The impact of the crash spun the van again, but this time, instead of me seeing things clearly, I was pinned.

"Let's go! Let's go!" Rubber yelled from outside of the van.

It was apparent that he was in the half that wasn't twisted all the way around, and Gunz's lifeless eyes were still wide open. I tried pushing myself from the position I was in but realized my left arm was stuck, and by the looks of it, it was under the overturned van. My adrenaline had kept me from feeling pain, but once I actually saw and realized that I wasn't going anywhere, I screamed.

"Ahhhh!!!"

Sirens could still be heard, but there was no movement. I looked over at Gunz again, closed my eyes, and tried to find Rubberhead. The shots firing around me told the story of two different caliber guns, and by the way several single rounds filled the air, I figured that Rubberhead was being fired on, just as he was firing at them.

"We got one still alive inside of the vehicle!" I could hear an officer yell.

My breathing quickened when trying to feel my hand. "Aahhhh!"

I couldn't move and couldn't turn to see where the cop was coming from. Boy, I knew I wasn't about to go out like the rest of them clowns that found themselves in front of a judge after spending a year and some in a hospital ward.

I found the handle of the assault rifle stock, pulled it to me, and called for Rubberhead. "Take it to they ass, Rubber! Take it—" Unable to see or hear the old head, I let off a round of shots. I was not going back to prison. Those were the words I continually told myself before everything around me went black. "I'm not going back," I whispered until my breath was no more.

Chapter Sixteen

Brent

It couldn't have been more than a couple of hours since I last heard from Daxx, but I was hoping like hell he was taking care of his business, because me having to continually check my windows for danger was something I wasn't used to. I was just about to walk out of my office when the tech I'd paid $500 to peeked his head into my office door.

"Hey, Boss, you might need to see this."

Seeing him hurry to grab the remote from my desk, I frowned, and before I could inquire of his actions, he flipped through the channels until he found the one he'd been searching for.

"Breaking news," he told me before pointing at the mounted flat screen.

I quickly read the caption, but what caught my attention more than anything was the footage shown—apparently taken from a chopper of the local news station.

"Turn it up. Turn it up." I immediately recognized the grey minivan I'd just had delivered not even three hours ago. It wasn't until I read and heard that one of the occupants was dead, one was critically injured, and one was at large that it hit me. "Oh, shit!"

I prayed that Daxx wasn't stupid enough to carry out the hit on his own, but when thinking about what was said recently, I couldn't think of anything else. I waited to see if there was any talk of the occupants being identified. All they kept saying was that there was a high-speed chase that ended with several shots being fired from the van seconds before it collided with another van and overturned after striking a wooden utility pole on the corner.

"Dammit, I hope this nigga ain't this stupid," I told myself before turning to the tech, who wore an expression that told me he had a concern of his own. I wasn't trying to make too much of it known in front of him, but I asked, "Did you wipe it down?"

"Yeah, yeah. I'm not tripping on that. I'm tripping because I saw the greedy niggas standing beside a Benz when I dropped it off."

"Was one of them Daxx?" He was sure to remember the face of the man who I'd cursed out plenty of times here at the shop. Hell, all of the guys working either here or at the lot knew Daxx.

"Yep. Him and two other guys. And they were all high as hell."

I lowered my head and closed my eyes. "Stupid ass nigga," I whispered. We both jumped when hearing my phone ring. I yanked it up, hoping like hell it was Daxx and that the shit he and his goons just did wasn't about to fall back on me. "Nigga, what the fuck!"

"Brent?"

Instead of Daxx, it was Sheila, and by the sound of her voice, she was just as worried as I was. "Are you watching the news, Brent?"

There was no way she would have known Daxx or I had anything to do with what was taking place on the news, and instead of multiplying her concern, I only asked, "Why, what's up?"

"They're talking about three men having a shootout with the police."

"Okay, what are you trippin' on?" I asked in a nonchalant way.

"Because it has Daxx written all over it. Earlier, they said something about the same suspects in the same van crashing into a building, and six known blood gang members getting killed."

I paused when hearing Sheila's assessment of it, because she was closer than the cops had come so far. Being that I caught the tail end of the newscast, I didn't catch that first part. I sighed. "I'm going to get back to you."

"And did you notice the dealer's tag on the van? It's one of yours."

Those words echoed in my ears long after ending the call with Sheila, because there it was. It was always said that before committing any crime, seven mistakes would have already been made, and me relying on others not to make them was the very one that I overlooked. How could either of them leave the dealer's plate on the rear of the van? Daxx promised that the van would be burned afterwards, but that never happened.

"Shit!"

It wouldn't be long before the cops came here asking questions about the van, but the one thing I had working in my favor was that I'd already reported it stolen. That was something I did as soon as the tech returned.

***

Raylon

After a few stops and collecting a few ends, I pulled into the parking lot of the LaQuinta Inn, spotted Cindy's Bentley mid-ways towards the back, and parked alongside it. The two kilos I was taking to the OKC were put away in the compartment, along with the $22,000 I'd picked up. I reached for my gun, seeing that it wouldn't be needed, and left it in the compartment also. I had one thing on my mind, and as soon as I was done with Cindy, I was on to my business elsewhere. I had to make sure I flipped the money I now had, because I'd been taking too many losses, and it was about time I came up with a win.

While making my way through the lobby and onto the elevator, I thought about my wife. I was going to bless her game as soon as I got my ass from out the sand. I'd lost her car fucking with some slick motherfuckers, but I knew I was slicker. The bait game was one we'd been playing for a minute, and if them motherfuckers thought I wasn't coming back, they had some more shit coming.

"I was beginning to worry," Cindy said while opening the door for me.

"For you, I'll always come," I told her before making my way inside. I smiled when seeing her naked, because she definitely knew how to greet a nigga, and she also knew what I wanted.

"Did you bring the work?"

"Yeah. I had to make a couple of stops and grab a little something from my workers." I slapped her ass as I passed her and looked towards the bathroom, expecting to see the light-complected chick named Carmine. I smiled at the memory, and after seeing mine, Cindy smiled also.

"Really?"

"Hey." I threw my hands up. "Everybody loves surprises."

"Well, maybe next time, because right now, I'm wanting you for myself."

I watched as Cindy crossed the room and began unbuckling my belt. I unbuttoned my shirt and allowed her to plant a trail of kisses from my chest to my stomach. I pulled her towards the bed.

"I ordered some pizza and a gyro sandwich, and they should be here in about thirty minutes."

"That gives me time to get in this ass, then," I told her before stepping out of my slacks and boxer briefs. I watched her smile when seeing the dick spring to the left, and the minute she reached for the pillow at the head of the bed, it brought a smile across my face as well.

"Put this under my ass, Raylon. Then flip me over. I want to feel you deep inside of me."

I held both of her thick legs up with one hand, and with the other, I placed the huge pillow under her, raising her ass and pussy to a position that allowed me to stimulate her G-spot. I bent down, sucked on her pearl tongue until it hardened, and spanked her with the dick. "Your black ass going to make me hurt you, Cindy."

"As long as it's with that dick, we all good." She laughed before reaching for each of her ankles.

The sight of her clean-shaved pussy alone had me leaking pre-cum, and when seeing her asshole clench, I placed the head of my dick at the entrance of her pussy and began squeezing her thighs. "Here, look. I want you to see this dick. I want you to see what you running from." I entered Cindy with short strokes until I'd lubricated the dick with her juices. I rocked her to the rhythm of my strokes until her toes curled and the soles of her feet wrinkled. "You like it like that?" I teased, using only half of the dick.

"Yeah, yeah, right there, Raylon. Keep it right there."

I fucked Cindy in that position alone until a thick lather of cum covered my dick and stomach. I fucked her until she trembled and her stomach heaved, and still hadn't given her the entire length of the dick. I pulled out, spanked her on the ass, and said, "Flip that shit over right quick."

"Damn, nigga. You trying to own this motherfucker, ain't you?"

"This is what I do," I told her before reaching for the other pillow and handing it to her. "I want that ass all the way up."

"Ughh, shit! Wait a minute."

The knock on the door came just in time, because once I got in her from behind, she was sure to run from the dick, and I wasn't going to stop. Some dude walked in, then a bad feeling hit me when I noticed who the heavyset guy was, because I'd seen him before. He was the same guy I'd bet and lost Shoney's car against in the OKC. I regarded him with narrow slits. This must've been a lick.

"You motherfuckers just practicing with me, because I don't have shit," I told them before looking back at Cindy.

"Nigga, I said thirty minutes!" Cindy yelled.

I looked back at Cindy, who was now climbing off of the bed herself. She was in on this shit. I closed my eyes and laughed.

"Sorry, Boss Lady, but when I heard you screaming, I thought—"

"Boss Lady?" I turned to face her again. Cindy was standing in the middle of the room naked.

"Yeah, that's what I am, Raylon, and these are my niggas. I just wish they would have waited a little while longer, because the dick was getting good, and you already know how hard it is to find some good dick out here."

Before I knew it, I was hit in the back of the head and pushed across the bed. My eyes went from Cindy to the heavyset guy.

"We already checked the truck, and he ain't got shit in it," said the short guy.

"Take it, anyway. I'm sure he has a compartment in it," she told them before making her way into the bathroom.

"What about this nigga? Do we kill him?"

When I spun to see the answer she gave, my mouth was covered with duct tape, and my hands were pulled behind me. “Ummm, mmmm!”

“Have we got the money out of the safe yet?” Cindy looked at him as if he was the dumbest nigga alive.

My thoughts went to my wife.

“Boss Lady, they inside.” I watched as he handed her his phone.

Hearing her name, I opened my eyes and watched her. She’d put back on her clothes and handed them mine. *Inside?*

“What’s up?” she asked whoever it was on the other end.

Cindy regarded me with slanted eyes and a slight smile. If I could have killed her ass, it would have been done in the most horrific way possible. The bitch had been playing me all along. I knew from the beginning that she knew more about me than she should have, but this was some more shit. I laid there and listened to her talk, and when hearing her speak of my wife, I shook my head vigorously.

“What’s the code to the safe, Raylon?”

Right then, the tape was snatched off my lips, and it felt as if my lips went with it. I mumbled, “What safe?”

“The one your black ass wife is standing in front of right now,” she told me.

“She ain’t got shit to do with this, Cindy. Leave her out of it.”

“She has everything to do with it, sweetheart. ‘Cause right now, she’s standing between me and the half a million dollars you got stashed there.”

The conversation that me and Cindy had just a week ago came to mind. That was right before the races and the day me and her hooked up to do what we’d been doing for a while now. I’d told her about the moves me and the boys were making, and the number did pop up somewhere.

“You can have all that shit. Just don’t hurt my wife, Cindy. Please.”

“The code.”

The thought of them doing to Shoney what had been done to some of the other wives I knew clouded my train of thought, as well as my vision. Someone violating my wife would definitely have me traveling the ends of the earth in pursuit of them. I said a silent prayer that they'd let her make it. Me giving them the code was the least in my mind. I could get all that back and smoke, but right now, Shoney was priority.

"1490," I mumbled with closed eyes.

"I really enjoyed the ride, Raylon, but like all things, it comes to an end."

"Do we kill him or what?" the short guy asked a second time.

I exhaled when Cindy smiled and walked out, and closed my eyes when they did the same. The bitch let me live. I struggled to free myself, but the bonds they put me in wouldn't bulge. I tired myself in the event, because I had to get to Shoney. I had to make sure she was all right. I had to.

***

Brent

I tried calling Raylon and tried contacting Daxx, but it was as if they didn't even exist. It was then when the thought came of them both trying to carry out the hit, as they'd done many times in the past. It was always that they'd done their dirt together, but lately, they'd been on some more shit, and I didn't even think they were still talking. Not after the day at Raylon's when Daxx had brought those goons to his home.

I walked from my office to the rear of the shop, hoping and praying that my boys were not caught up in the shit that was happening on the television. They did some outlandish things at times, but this one, by far, surpassed all else.

"Where the fuck these niggas at?" I continually asked myself after being sent to the voicemail on both of their phones.

***

Shoney

Even before pulling into my driveway, I knew something was off. Sept had my mind in a million different places, and the thoughts I was having put more than a weight on my shoulders and worry in my heart. The woman was becoming something I couldn't identify.

"Did you leave the door open, Sept?" I asked when seeing the glass doors to my patio opened and half of the curtain spilled out.

"Nope. Ya man probably got some tramp up there."

"Bullshit," I told her, knowing he wasn't that damn crazy. I looked for either his truck or some other car belonging to a woman. There was neither. "That nigga ain't that stupid, Sept. I promise you that." I parked in my usual spot and climbed out. I wasn't about to be one of them dumb ass women on the scary movies that go into the house asking a ton of unanswered questions, and I damn sure wasn't about to sit at the bottom of no stairs listening to my husband and some bitch fucking. I looked over at Sept and said, "Give me your gun right quick."

"You sure?"

Instead of answering, I reached for the .380 and clicked off the safety feature. I knew to do that much at least. "If someone is in my house, they about to get a couple of holes in they ass."

"Let's go," Sept agreed. She followed close behind me.

We made our way into the patio doors, and I stopped when having to step over the overturned statue I kept there. My mouth fell open when seeing that whoever was there had fucked up all my shit. I found myself pointing the small pistol in front of me.

"The cops are on the way, so whoever you are, you'd better find the nearest exit!" Sept yelled from behind me.

Sept and I walked through the entire house twice, and each time, I was really hoping I found someone hiding under something or in one of the many closets we had. We both ended up in the one place that wasn't rummaged through: the kitchen.

"They tore up my house, Sept," I told her once I was sure no one else was there, and I'd given her back her gun.

"Just be glad you weren't here, Shoney."

"Hell, if I was here, they wouldn't have done this shit," I told her.

"If you were here, you might have been stretched out over one of the couches or in the bathtub dead, Shoney. Whoever did this shit had it on their mind."

"They might have even been watching the house and saw when we left before doing this." I tried to put the pieces together, but this wasn't some shit I did, and it damn sure wasn't no TV program. "The safe!" I screamed before running up the stairs. They had to have been looking for something, and sure as shit stinks and gets pushed out of an ass, Raylon's safe was open, and by the looks of it, the code was entered instead of it being broken into.

"They took all the money, Sept."

"Girl, fuck that money. We good."

I watched my girl incredulously. Raylon was going to have a fit when he found out. I turned when hearing Sept laugh, and frowned when seeing the smile spread across her face.

"The money they got was counterfeit, Shoney."

"What?"

"It was fake. That's what I'd been doing for the longest, Shoney. I was swapping counterfeit for real," she told me.

"You what?"

"I'd been buying counterfeit from Jacoby and replacing the shit with the money Raylon had in the safe. We been doing that for the longest. Don't act like you didn't know, Shoney."

I followed Sept out through the patio door and sat across from her in the lawn chair. "That's how you got all of that money?"

"Yep, and it's apparent that's what they came looking for. Ain't no telling what that nigga out there doing, Shoney. I'm just glad we hit his ass before they got the chance to."

I thought about what Sept said and looked from her to the entrance of my driveway. For that much money, they would have definitely done something to me if I was here.

"They came to my house, Sept."

"And they could have killed you and that nigga. Motherfuckers out here playing for keeps, Shoney. Whoever did that shit been on it for a minute. They knew where you lived and the code to the safe. That ain't luck."

"Call Brent while I call the police," I told her before pulling out my phone.

"For what? So you can tell the cops some motherfuckers broke in and took a shit load of counterfeit money? Girl, fuck that. What we need to be doing is packing your shit."

"Raylon isn't answering, Sept," I told her, having called him three times already.

"Does he ever? Especially when he out doing some shit he ain't supposed to be doing. Brent will show before that nigga will."

While Sept dialed Brent's number, I made my way back inside to see what else was taken. We'd already come to the conclusion that whoever it was that robbed my home knew what they were coming for, and I was hoping like hell it didn't have shit to do with me or the things I did in the past.

Chapter Seventeen

Raylon

For over an hour, I fought at the restraints they put me in. One of the guys had turned the volume sky high on the television, and my muffled screams went no farther than the room I was in. I sighed and did my best to make my presence known when hearing the housekeeper outside of the room door. Someone must have complained about the television being so high, and I was thankful, because without them, I might have been there all night.

With no response to his knocking, the keeper used his key card to open the door, and by the way he froze when seeing me bound and gagged on the bed naked, I was praying he didn't turn and run.

"Hey, man. Are you alright?"

I vigorously moved my head from side to side while he slowly approached me.

"You ain't in here on no freaky shit, are you?"

I tried to smile but still shook my head to disagree. When seeing him walk towards the television and decrease its volume, I rolled my eyes, and the minute he freed me from the bondage I was in, I told him, "Thanks, man. You're a lifesaver."

"Man, you're like the third nigga I found strung up like that," he told me while looking in the adjoining room and bath.

Instead of entertaining his dumb ass, I snatched the phone up and dialed Brent. I had to make sure someone went to see about my wife.

***

Shoney

To my surprise, only our things were broken, and as much glass as I had around my house, I was sure there would have been so much more to clean up. For the most part, things were overturned, which let me know that it was the safe they were looking for, and cabinets were left open. And after calming myself as best I could, and being consoled by both Sept and Brent, I was finally able to sit down and think this shit through to where I was straightening furniture, replacing pillows, and aligning pictures while Sept was trying to put my belongings in boxes. She was really packing my shit.

"I'm not letting you stay here another night, Shoney." Sept walked downstairs with two suitcases filled with my personal things and handed them to Brent, who was more than happy to oblige her.

"She's right, Shoney. This shit is crazy right now, and your safety is what matters most. Fuck this house," Brent told me before walking my things to the foyer area.

"Can I just sit and think for a minute, y'all?" I stood, placed my hands on my hips, and closed my eyes. I was being pulled and pushed in two different directions.

"Think about what?"

"I—" Before I could form the words, Brent's phone rang, and when seeing him hold up his finger, silencing us, I knew it had to be my husband.

"Whoa, whoa, whoa. What are you talking about?"

Both Sept and I could hear Raylon yell through the phone. We listened, and as soon as Brent tried to walk off and conduct his talk in private, Sept and I grabbed him.

"They got Shoney, Brent. I need you to go make sure my wife is okay!"

"Who got Shoney?" Brent asked while looking back at me.

My expression matched his, because I didn't know what the hell he was talking about either.

"They went to my house, Brent. The bitch lured me out here to the hotel while her goons hit my shit, and Shoney was there."

"Raylon—"

"They told me if I didn't give them the code to the safe they'd hurt her. I gave them what they wanted, Brent. I gave them—"

"Raylon, slow down, nigga. Slow down!"

"Cindy. Cindy. That bitch set me up."

"Where are you at, Raylon?"

"At the hotel, nigga. Them hoes took my shit, my truck, my clothes, and my money."

I felt my heart sink and shatter at the same time, because this was my husband I was listening to talk about how some bitch set him up, when really he set himself up for the shit. He'd been still fucking over me even after he promised he'd stop. His doing so could have placed me in a situation I wouldn't have known how to deal with. I turned and walked away from the both of them. Sept followed.

"That's what his ass gets, Shoney. That's what his punk ass gets," Sept continued to chant, seeing me getting pulled into anxiety, hurt, anger, and everything else you felt when your heart broke because of your man.

"They could have killed him, September," I told her, expressing my concern for him, even though I was still hurting like hell.

"They should have killed his ass. That stupid ass nigga always think a bitch want some dick. Bitches are out here playing for keeps, Shoney."

"Sept, please," I pleaded while wiping tears from my yes.

It was bad enough that people had come to my house, and to hear that he was elsewhere meeting up with some bitch was too much. I looked towards where my bags were packed, thought about snatching the phone from Brent, and giving Raylon a piece of my mind, but thought better of it. Hell, it was good that he'd thought I was in some danger. Danger that he'd brought up on me.

"I'm on my way," I heard Brent say before ending the call.

Sept and I watched as he headed up the stairs and returned with some clothes for my husband. I knew the shit wasn't funny, but somehow, I managed a smile.

"I wouldn't have taken his ass nothing. I would have made his ass run to the car with a sheet wrapped around his ass and prayed like hell the management would have taken that from him," Sept told him before he left.

I turned towards Sept and thought how she'd be capable of doing something like this. It was always that she continually warned me against the things Raylon had done and how he'd eventually bring harm to me. It was always that she was spot on when it came to the things my husband was doing. It was as if Sept had been playing and planning this for the longest.

I waited until Brent was gone before telling her, "They came to my house, Sept. How did they know where I lived in the first place?" I took a seat on the sofa and watched her.

"That nigga ain't hard to find, Shoney. I wouldn't be surprised if he brought one of them hoes here himself. That's how stupid he is."

"Why didn't they come when I was here? Why did they wait until I went to the courthouse with you before breaking in my home?" I wiped tears from my eyes for the third time, and when seeing her without answer, I asked, "Did you do this, September?"

"Do what?"

"Have my husband set up and my home robbed?" I had to ask. I had to.

"Don't start that shit, black ass woman. Point the finger at that pile of shit you can't see past. If I was behind the shit, I would have bled his ass a long time ago, and I damn sure wouldn't have been sneaking around here with your scary ass stealing his money, Shoney. You say some of the dumbest shit sometimes, you know that?"

I sat, listened, and watched my girl go off like she always did when I accused her of something, and if nothing else, I knew she was being truthful with me. I knew she didn't have shit to do with Raylon being unfaithful, but her having the code to his safe was questionable. But still, I felt I had to ask.

"That Cindy bitch played the cards he dealt her, and she trumped the nigga. Plain and simple. He was thinking with his dick, and she was thinking with much, much more. I wish I did have a bitch like that on my arm."

Quiet as kept, she did. I'd sat and talked to Reniya personally and knew it was in her to put her pussy on a man's hand. Hell, she'd done it twice already. The only thing was, she hadn't yet learned how to separate the emotions she had from the game she played.

"And another thing," Sept said as we were walking my belongings out to my truck. "It will stay between us. As far as Raylon is concerned, y'all broke, you hear me, Shoney? You ain't about to give that nigga shit."

If it wasn't for Sept, that story would have been true. We would have been broke, and I would have, once again, been depending on Raylon to do for me. I nodded in agreement. I'd never go through that again. When seeing her climb into my truck, I stopped her, threw her the key fob to my CLS, and told her, "We ain't leaving the Benz, Sept. We are not leaving my Benz."

***

Brent

As soon as I entered the parking lot of the hotel, I spotted Raylon on the balcony wrapped in a white sheet. He frantically waved me down from where he stood. Under any other circumstances, I would have made his ass do just what Sept suggested, but I was glad to see him alive and away from the spotlight Daxx and his team had put above themselves.

I hurried into the building, and as soon as the elevator door opened, Raylon was standing there. I handed him a pair of jeans, a t-shirt, and a pair of his sneakers. "Here."

"Did you go by to check on Shoney or what?"

I followed Raylon in the suite and looked around. I saw torn pieces of duct tape and a disheveled bed. "Have you been looking at the news, nigga?"

"Man, fuck the news. I'm worried about my wife."

I watched as Raylon dressed himself. "Sorry, I didn't think to bring you any boxers. But I was in a rush," I told him.

"The bitch set me up, Brent. All this time I was fucking that black ass woman, she was running a play on a nigga."

Raylon stepped into his shoes and was headed out of the door when I told him, "Shoney knows everything, Raylon. She was there with me when you called."

"They said they had her at the house and that—"

"They played you, Ray. By the time Shoney and Sept got there, the robbers had already taken off."

I saw the relief spread across Raylon's face—saw him deflate when hearing that his wife had heard everything from beginning to end, and once I told him that I had helped her and Sept pack some of her belongings, he only closed his eyes.

"I swear, I'm going to kill that bitch, Brent. Them hoes took me for everything, man."

"Naw, what you're going to do is sit your ass down somewhere. We're not putting Shoney through anything like this again." I walked from where I stood toward the television and flipped through the channels, hoping something would be said to ease him up. "Have you seen the shit on the news that's going on out here?"

"I should have known the bitch was up to something. What did Shoney say when she heard that shit, Brent? What did she—"

"Cried, nigga. Ya wife sat there and cried her eyes out, man. You fucked up now, Raylon. You really did," I told him.

"I'm going to take care of it. I got Shoney."

I didn't answer, because although she was his wife, it was evident that he wasn't hearing anything I'd just said. "We might have a hell of a lot more shit to deal with," I told him.

"Like what?"

I ran it down to Raylon the way I saw it, and after telling him that I had a strong feeling Daxx was involved personally, we both just sat there.

"The newswoman said that one of the assailants was still at large."

"And you think that's Daxx?" he asked, remaining hopeful also.

"Only one way to find out. Call the county jail or the hospital."

"Even if he dies or some shit like that, I doubt if he'd have his ID on him. He might have been running with them renegade ass dope fiends, but I doubt he'd do some stupid shit like that."

I paced the floor of the room and told him, "And you out here on some dumb shit too. What if something would have happened to that girl? Then what?"

"Man, I got Shoney. I can get all that other shit back. She knows that."

"I hope like hell Daxx ain't went and got himself killed, Raylon."

"As long as you reported the van stolen, you good," he said while following me out the door and onto the elevator.

"So, what are we going to do now?" I asked, seeing him in thought.

"I'm going to stop by Sheila's so I can get some more work. I've got to make this money back."

"Seriously, Raylon? You've got to be kidding me right now. Your wife needs you, and you are talking about trying to make some money back? You fucked up for real, nigga."

"Nigga, I'm broke now! I've got to put this shit back together, Brent."

Sept was right, and as bad as I hated to admit it, Raylon didn't deserve Shoney. He never did, and until he was shown just that, he'd always see what he wanted to see. But for right now, it was time we saw about Daxx.

Chapter Eighteen

Daxx

Two days later

The rhythmic beeping of the monitors was the first song I heard once I came to, and seeing the two uniformed guards standing at the entrance of the door pulled me all the way out of the anesthetic-induced slumber. My head hurt like hell, and the tubing placed down my throat had my mouth dryer than a motherfucker.

"He's finally awake," said one of the guards.

I tried to raise myself, but the pain that shot through my chest and ribs halted me. "Shit."

"Hey, man, just be still."

I looked up at the young white cop and nodded.

"You're lucky to be alive," he told me seconds before a nurse and doctor walked in.

I could only watch as they checked the monitors and documented the reasons I couldn't move. When hearing that I'd suffered from head trauma, a couple of broken ribs, and a punctured lung, my thoughts took me back to the accident itself. But after being told that half of my arm had to be amputated because of the injury I suffered when the van tilted and fell on it, I literally shut down.

I'd lost so much blood that I'd passed out, and it wasn't until days later did I regain consciousness. As soon as the doctor left the room, both of the cops took turns playing the aftermath of what had taken place. When they spoke of the guy that died, I knew they were talking about Gunz, because I did remember his lifeless body being thrown back and forth as I wrestled with the steering of the van. I also knew Rubberhead was still at large, and for the life of me, I couldn't understand that. That nigga had more than nine lives.

"But why am I handcuffed to this bed?" I managed to ask, hoping it wasn't as bad as it seemed for me.

"Dude, are you serious? You guys killed six motherfuckers before the cops got in behind you, and one of the guys in the rear of the van opened fire on them."

I laid there with my eyes closed while it all came back together. I knew I'd shot at least two guys and a woman and damn near ran over another, but I didn't have shit to do with shooting at no cops.

"You're so far up shit's creek, God can't reach you," said the other cop.

I looked over at what was left of my left arm for the first time. The forearm and hand were gone, and the bandage that covered it would need to be changed soon. I looked up at the ceiling and exhaled. Just last week, I was copping a brand-new Benz off the showroom floor, and today, I was laid up in a hospital room realizing that my life was over. I'd gotten so far into this shit that it was no turning back.

"Did they tell you about the shit load of drugs you had in your system? That was the only thing that kept you alive, man," the officer told me before checking my restraints a second time.

This was exactly what I didn't want, but here I was, and no one was to blame but me. I hated like hell that Gunz fucked around and had gotten himself killed, but me being in the state I was in at the moment wasn't that much better.

I thought about what the cop had said about Rubber and asked, "Did any cops get killed?"

"Three were shot, but they're going to be okay. We know you didn't do the shooting, so you're good on that end of the turd."

I smiled when seeing them smile at me. It wasn't because I understood the humor in their words. It was because I wished it was their asses that took the hot ones. That, and the fact that Rubber had gotten away. Now all I had to do was get me a good lawyer, a bond, and vacation. I'd come back and put this shit back together later.

***

Shoney

For the past couple of days, I'd either been ignoring Raylon's calls or listening to him and Sept argue and fight because of it. Despite me knowing for a fact that he was at some hotel with a bitch, he still swore they'd met up to discuss money and more bets he was sure to gain from. The nigga even had a lie to tell when I asked why Brent needed to bring him some clothes.

As always, I just wanted my husband to be truthful with me, but that wasn't about to happen anytime soon. And on top of that, he hadn't been staying at the house, either, and that was something Brent slipped and told September just last night. The last place the nigga would have been was in some hotel room alone, and I was more than sure he was with some other hoe, but I was through with his shit. Raylon Edwards wasn't ever going to change.

For nights, I'd stayed up worried about him going off to do something stupid or retaliating against the people that robbed our home, as well as hoping he wasn't with some other woman, because I did still love my husband. But I wasn't about to be sucked into the shit he had going on. Reality had set in, and I could have easily been killed in the event. If not that, I could have been seriously hurt because of the shit Raylon had going on, and as much as I tried to voice that, he continually spoke of the shit being over and that I didn't have to worry about it anymore. He was steady lying to me, and I was tired.

The only reason I came to work today was to get out of the house and to get my mind off of him, and that was the hardest thing for me to do. But when he showed up at my job with the same lies he'd already been exposed with, I didn't know what to do.

"Just leave the woman alone, Raylon. Damn," Sept told him when seeing that I couldn't get him to leave.

"Stay out of my business, Sept," he told her.

Instead of allowing them to cause a bigger scene, I grabbed Raylon's arm and led him outside. It was already enough that my co-workers saw that Raylon and I were at odds, and I didn't need them knowing exactly what it was about.

"Weak ass!" I heard Sept mumble.

"Stop lying to me, Raylon. I don't deserve this shit." I looked deep into his eyes, and when seeing the same things I'd seen for years, I turned from him.

"Babe, I'm not. Just come home tonight so we can talk about this. Shoney, please."

"Talk about what, Raylon? Some of the same shit I've been trying to talk to you about for years?"

Raylon grabbed my arm, felt me pulling back, and stepped into me. He wrapped his strong arms around me, kissed my forehead and my lips. "I need you, Shoney. I need you at home with me. I haven't slept in days, and I'm fucked up with myself right now. I love you, babe. Please."

"I can't keep doing this, Raylon. What happens the next time some bitch you're fucking robs you, huh?"

"I was not fucking that woman, Shoney. That bitch set the shit up to make it look as if I was, but we both know I wasn't fucking that stank ass woman."

"I just need some time, Raylon. Let me think about this for a few more days."

"Please, Shoney. I need you to make love to me. I need to feel you beside me and to know that you're alright."

By the time Raylon climbed into his car and pulled off, I'd broken. I knew what I wasn't going to do was tell him that I had all of his money safely stashed away. Sept would never forgive me if I did that. After composing myself and fixing my clothes, I headed back inside wearing a smile. I shouldn't have headed straight to September's cubicle.

***

September

"I don't want to hear that weak ass shit, Shoney." Here I was, calling myself having her back when it came to that sorry ass nigga she called a husband, and she went and reneged on everything we'd talked about and promised. I was the only one praying she had the strength to stay away from this nigga, and as much as she swore she would, I should have known it was something said to appease me. There was no coming between Shoney and that nigga, and my stupid ass continually found that out after every fight they had. Shoney was just like all them other bitches that couldn't see past the dick. Didn't want to feel shit but the dick and felt it was their fault when another bitch was getting that same dick. "Sad. You are so sad, Shoney."

"Just listen, Sept. It's only for tonight. Me not being home might have brought him to his senses. He knows I'm not about to keep going through this mess, Sept."

"Yeah, whatever." I typed some shit I wasn't even reading. Shoney had me so fucked up. All the begging and pleading I'd done didn't mean shit to her, especially after that nigga dun promised her something we all knew wouldn't be kept or done. All that no-good ass nigga had to do was touch her black ass, and she'd melt and turn into one of the stupidest motherfuckers alive.

"I'm telling you, Sept. I'm not moving back in until I see something different."

I half laughed, because not only had she said the same things before, but I was the one that suggested the idea on too many occasions to remember. I looked past Shoney towards our supervisor's office. That punk motherfucker disappeared the minute Raylon walked his ass in the door. "Mr. Dillan, can you please come get your employee?! She's keeping me from my work!" I screamed loud enough for the entire office to here.

"I promise, Sept. I'm not going to tell him anything about the money. I promise."

"Once that nigga starts fucking you, you're going to tell him more than that. You keep on talking about he ain't going to change, but you ain't, either. You the one ain't going to change, Shoney." I shooed her with my free hand and said, "Get away from my cubicle so I can finish working."

"Let me perform, Sept. It'll come to an end."

"Um, whatever." I thought about the many niggas I either fucked or let fuck with the pussy. I could still count on one hand how many of them niggas actually got the pussy for free. And when thinking about it, two of them niggas didn't even count. "Dick ain't never done me like that," I mumbled under my breath.

***

Raylon

Once I'd gotten things straightened out with my wife and made a few stops, I headed to Asia's because I had to pick up some more work, and this was where I'd been spending my nights. Now that Daxx was laid up under armed security in the hospital, I was having to piece the puzzle back together as best I could. He'd been fucking over both workers and clientele alike, and I was now having to make the shit ring.

By the time I pulled into Asia's driveway, it was already on my mind that I was about to fuck her yellow ass down. After some promises and a little begging last night, she finally gave in and gave me the pussy. I knew most of the reason was because she knew Shoney had left me, and the other reason was that she wanted me all for herself. And after hearing that I'd gotten robbed by Cindy and her goons from the OKC, or wherever it was they were from, she knew I needed a shoulder to lean on, some hot pussy, and her king's treatment.

"Is everything alright, Raylon?"

I walked past Asia and headed into the back room. "Take that shit off. You know what time it is."

"You didn't get enough last night, babe?"

When I did return from the back, Asia was standing in front of the entertainment center I'd spent $2,500 for, naked. I walked to her, grabbed her by both her fifty-inch hips, and pulled her to me. I knelt, kissed her stomach, and made her spread her legs. This pussy tasted like marshmallows.

"Umm."

It didn't take much for Asia's clit to get erect, and as soon as it did, I pulled her onto the floor, sliding my hands under her shoulders so she couldn't run from the dick, and eased it into her.

"Oh my god! Raylon."

At first, I thought she was just bullshitting me when she talked about not having vaginal intercourse for so long, but when feeling how tight her pussy was, there was no question in my mind that she'd been saving the pussy.

"Throw it back, babe," I coached her the way I coached my wife.

"I can't, Ray! Damn!"

I could feel the coolness on her tongue, having sucked air through her teeth, and to ease her into the transition, I took her bottom lip into my mouth, sped up my stroke, and went a little deeper.

"This pussy feels like heaven," I told her, knowing what it did to my wife when I told her how good her pussy was to me.

"Shut up, Raylon."

"I'm serious, Asia," I told her while giving deeper and slower strokes. Once I got her to take all of me, I held it there, waited until she initiated the movement, and matched her. I raised slightly so she could wind and grind under me. I kissed her deeply, and when feeling her wrap her legs around me, I reached down, palmed both of her ass cheeks, locked my chin on her right shoulder, and fucked her with long, fast strokes. The sound of my thighs smacking against the bottom of her ass could be heard over the moans and grunts we made, and the deeper I went, the louder the farts her pussy made. "This is my pussy now, Asia."

"Slow down, Raylon! Slow..."

Seeing her begin to tremble, I raised myself, placed her right leg on my shoulder, and looked down to see the pussy cum. It might have been my second time getting me some pussy from her, but I knew her body already. I knew what she liked and what made her respond in ways she hadn't with anyone else.

"Make it bite, babe. Make that pussy bite!" I urged her with short, quick strokes.

While fucking Asia, I thought about Cindy and all the ways I fucked her. There was no way she could stay away from me, and if she ever showed her face again, she had this coming.

***

Brent

It didn't take long for me to find Daxx, and after arguing with both of the guards for damn near ten minutes and coming off $1,000, I was allowed to see hm.

"I am immediate family," I told the nurse before entering.

Daxx was already looking towards the door when I entered. Tears were in his eyes, but he still managed a weak smile. "What up, Big Boy?"

"Ten minutes," the officer told us before sitting down in the chair right outside the open door.

I looked Daxx over, noticed all of the bandages and tubes, and shook my head. I told him, "Look at the shit you done to yourself, yellow ass nigga."

"I'm fucked up, huh?"

"Fucked up ain't the word. Can you even move, nigga?" I stretched out the monitor, and that's when I noticed the handcuffs on his right hand.

"This ain't the half of it, Brent." Daxx held what was left of his left arm up and closed his eyes.

I found myself about to ask where the rest of it was, and that's when blood had begun to soak through the bandages. "You alright, nigga? Damn."

"I'll be fine, nigga. What I need to do now is get a damn lawyer, because as soon as the doctors think I'm good enough to stand, I'm going to jail, and I don't plan on being there that long. Not like this." He, again, held up his arm.

"Nigga, you'd better hope you make it to the jail, having shot at the cops and all the shit y'all did," I told him and looked back towards the doorway.

I still hadn't told Daxx about our other problem. Well, his problem, because he was dealing with so much as it was, but once he inquired about it, I couldn't lie to him.

"Then I'm going to need you to go get my money out of my account just in case the feds get in on this investigation."

"Um, what money, and which account?" I asked. It was hard to find the right words.

"Nigga, my money in both the accounts Sheila opened for me."

"Sheila's gone, Daxx, and the accounts have been closed," I told him before walking around to where I didn't have to move the machine around him.

"What you mean, she gone?"

"She caught out, thinking this shit was going to fall back on her, I guess. I talked to her the other day when we first saw the shit on the news. I tried to tell her that you didn't have shit to do with it, but I guess she found out otherwise."

"You've got to be shitting me, Brent. I had a half a million dollars in them accounts. All my shit was in the banks, Brent."

I shushed Daxx before he could get any louder. I told him, "She did leave a text saying that she'd forward the money into our shell and business accounts once the smoke cleared."

By the look on his face, it was apparent that he was thinking she was making sure she was clear of any wrongdoing, as well as making sure Daxx did not implicate her in anything. We all did.

"I need that money, Brent."

"Man, fuck that money. We've got plenty of shit to worry about besides that."

"I can't believe this shit, nigga. Have you heard from Rubberhead?"

"I got you. Don't worry about that shit right now. Fucking around with them niggas damn near got you killed."

I ran down some of the things pertaining to Raylon's misfortune, just to let him know that he wasn't the only one that fucked up. Told him that I'd more than likely be put under some kind of scope and that if that time ever came, I was going to close down shop and go under the radar for a little while.

"Bring it to a close, guys," said one of the guards.

"You act like I'm going to help motherfuckers flip the rocks or something."

"I ain't said shit about you snitching, nigga. I'm just say that if them feds come fucking with me, I'm going to pull back," I told him, knowing his mind was all over the place.

I didn't think he'd turn state or information on a nigga, but he was in deep shit, and he did know all of our business.

"Get on top of the lawyer for me, Brent. I'll call you when I land."

Outside, I looked over the text Sheila had left days ago. There was no mention of sending any money, but I had to use what I had at the time. I promised myself that I wasn't going to be on the ass end of things when they did backfire, and I was now having to do every and anything to ensure it. Knowing that I was about to be out of at least $60,000, I called Peter and the same bondsman I called when Sept got arrested.

***

Raylon

Once I'd made a few stops and checked on four of the six spots we'd been running work out of for the longest, I was on my way. After speaking with a few of the guys and hearing their versions when it came to Daxx, it didn't have to be said that some of them wished the worst for him, but for the most part, what they worried about was them not being supplied as we once did.

I counted over $50,000 and still had a kilo and a half, which let me know that Daxx had been manipulating the numbers for a while. The minute I pulled up to the light and stopped, a warm feeling washed over me. I subtly checked each mirror, looking for the obvious, hoping that there wasn't anybody staking my moves or knowing that I had so much money and drugs on me at the time, and noticed the same SUV I'd seen after leaving Asia's house.

At first, I thought nothing of it, but now that I was all the way across town seeing the same vehicle, my mind went into overdrive. What stood out about it were the short antennas on the roof and the mirrored tint on the windshield. I reached for the secret compartment but realized I was yet to have one installed in the CTS.

"Shit."

As soon as the light turned, I cut across two lanes so I could make the wild U-turn, and when seeing the SUV attempt to do the same, my suspicions were confirmed. I pulled my .40 cal from under the armrest, thumbed off the safety, and floored the Cadillac. At that instance, it seemed as if flashing lights came from everywhere. I counted two more SUVs, a town car, and a couple of cruisers, and they were boxing me in. Seeing no immediate way out, I slowed, pulled to the side of the street, and hit the steering wheel.

"This shit can't be happening," I told myself before hitting the infotainment center and dialing Brent. I sat for a few minutes it seemed like before either of the detectives approached the car. As soon as Brent came on the line, I exhaled and told him, "They got me, Brent."

"Who? What are you talking about now, Ray?"

"These motherfucking laws, nigga. They got me hemmed up right now." I watched through both my side mirrors as they approached from both sides. "Don't say shit, Brent. Here we go," I told him while lowering my driver's side window.

"Is there a problem, sir?" I asked loud enough for Brent to hear and understand my situation better.

"Um, we have reason to believe you have drugs in the car," said the cop.

"Drugs?" I frowned, leaned away from him, and shook my head. "You must have the wrong car, sir." While seeing him act as if contemplating his next move, a call came through on his shoulder piece, and I heard my name. My full name, matter of fact.

"You mind if I see your driver's license and registration, please?"

I thought about all the cash I had in that compartment and that the registration papers were under it somewhere. I didn't prepare for this trip at all, and it was now evident.

The minute I leaned over to act as if I was searching for the papers, he said, "Just step out of the car, Mr. Edwards," and by the way his hand hovered over the butt of his service weapon, no other move would have been accepted.

The ride downtown took longer than it should have, and when seeing them pull into the lot of the federal building, I knew it was about to be some shit. The money they found would more than likely be short once it hit the table, and filed as evidence against me, and the drugs would more than likely be put back on the streets, and that's why I felt I had a chance when it came to being given a charge I couldn't stand up under.

I was led to the exact same room I was taken to the last time I got caught up when traveling to Oklahoma, and to see the same detective enter the room wearing a smile on his face, I closed my eyes.

"Nice to see you again, Mr. Edwards. I'm hoping we can work together and make some of these charges disappear."

"Possession of a controlled substance, possession of a felony firearm. I know what the charges are," I told him, having been through the same shit before.

"How about we add, conspiracy to distribute and possession with the intent to distribute heroin and cocaine? 'Winter white'—as you call it."

"Those charges were dropped," I told him, knowing it was about to be some shit in the game.

"Yeah, thanks to Shoney. But that was then, and this is now."

I watched him walk from where he stood over to the chair across from me and sit. He slid a thick file towards me and nodded.

"What we caught you with are crumbs compared to what you're bringing out of Reynosa."

"Reynosa?" I frowned. There was no way he'd know about Reynosa unless someone in my circle had told him. I immediately thought about Daxx. I needed to know more. "What does Reynosa have to do with me and my arrest?"

"Mr. Edwards, we have recorded conversations with you detailing your transactions in Reynosa. We have dates, names, and routes. We know about the cartel, so if you choose to play this little game you're playing, you will lose."

I sat and listened to the evidence they had against me, but not one time did they mention Daxx, the gambling, the detail shop, the car lot, or any of the other things I had going on. All they wanted to know was about my partner across the border. They somehow knew more than they should have, but for the life of me, I couldn't see how. There was no plea deal offered, and as far as I could tell, they wanted my ass on a fruit-filled platter, along with the connect I'd purchased from the longest.

"I guess this means I got to get me a lawyer and fight it out in court," I told him.

"I'm going to give you a little time to reconsider that, Mr. Edwards."

Chapter Nineteen

Shoney

A week had passed since Raylon's arrest, and because he had priors for the same thing and wasn't willing to cooperate with federal detectives, he was given no bond and a federal detainer. It was not looking good for my husband at all. Since then, I'd moved back in with September, because I didn't need the feds suspecting me of any wrongdoings, and spending any amount of money was something I was very cautious of.

I'd been to visit Raylon every day, and after each one, we'd end up arguing and fighting because of the shit he was wanting me to do. If it wasn't one thing, it was another when it came to Raylon, but you couldn't tell him that.

I had been seated in the visitation booth wondering what was taking Raylon so long, and was praying he hadn't gotten in any trouble, because he'd normally be walked out in a matter of minutes. I smiled when seeing him being escorted through the doors. I stood.

"Hey, babe. You think about what I said?"

The smile I wore faded when hearing that, because here I was trying to better the situation, but here he was trying to make it worse. "Are you serious, Raylon?" I looked around to see who might have been in earshot, then looked back to my husband.

"Babe, I need you to get at Oscar for me. We need some cash, Shoney."

I still hadn't told him about the money I was sitting on, and as promised, I wouldn't. It was taking all of me not to mention it, but now that it was a possibility the feds were watching me, I couldn't change it. Brent even said that it was only so much he was willing to do for Raylon for not wanting to be put under the scope of the law. This would be one of those things Raylon had to deal with as best he could, and because he'd put the entire circle under fire on numerous occasions, now there was really nothing we could do if we wanted to stay clear of the things he and Daxx had going on.

"I'm not about to involve myself with that shit, Raylon. I'll help with the lawyers, bring you money, and be here for you through whatever, but I am not about to be some cellmate."

"We in this shit together, Shoney, remember?"

"Yeah. I also remember you saying we'd put this shit behind us once you got on your feet."

"I know you got some money put up somewhere, Shoney. I need you to make this happen for me."

"There's nothing I can do, Raylon. I don't have any connects to give up like I did the last time. Hell, I don't even know anybody that buys the shit anymore."

"What about them niggas that September be fucking with? I know they hustling."

"Their business is not mine, Raylon. I haven't the slightest idea what it is they do, if they're doing anything at all."

"Well, somebody in our business, because these motherfuckers know damn near everything about me and the shit I had going on. You must have told September something, and she ran and told them. How else would they have known about all the shit that I do?"

"How the hell would I know, Raylon?"

"This shit ain't happen by coincidence, Shoney. Somebody saying something."

By the time I left from visiting with Raylon, I was beyond upset. For him to accuse me of causing his arrest not only slapped me across the face, but told me that he was not trusting the things I said when it came to me telling Sept anything. For all I knew, it could have been Daxx or any of them dope fiends he had working for him. I was tired of his shit, and I did let him know as much.

***

Daxx

Regardless of my injury, as soon as I was able to stand on my own, I was discharged and transferred to the county jail. I was now charged with three counts of capital murder and kidnapping. There was no plea, and the only thing I kept hearing was the death penalty.

Come to find out, a couple of the guys holed up in that spot were under the age of seventeen, and the guy we'd kidnapped was a youngster. The lawyer Brent hired was pushing for a speedy trial, because it seemed the more time the prosecutor was given, the more evidence they were finding against me.

Them niggas I was supplying were telling shit they shouldn't have been, because they were also facing possession charges. One of the spots got ran on, because minutes after Raylon's arrest, the cops went back to the last place they'd followed him from. The same motherfuckers I was feeding were the same ones willing to testify against me. I knew that once some of this shit was heard in court, it would be over with for me. I'd asked Brent about the money that I at one time had, and he only told me that he'd take care of it. I knew that bitch had taken off with my money, and he was just saying some shit to make me feel better. My life was over, and I knew it.

"Give me something, Daxter. Make some of this shit go away," was what I was told, but I knew better.

On top of this was the fact that I was given no bond, and my lawyer was trying to find a way for me to get life without the possibility of parole, as if that was something to look forward to. The only thing I had working in my favor was that Rubberhead hadn't been caught yet. Evidence of that was when the deputy police chief visited me and kept asking who the son of a bitch was that was shooting his officers. One thing I promised myself was that I wasn't going back, but by the looks of it, that's exactly where I was headed. And in the condition I was in, and the people I'd either fucked over or had fucked off, I wasn't going to last a year. I had to make this shit go away as fast as I could.

***

Raylon

"Fat ass nigga!"

That motherfucker would have still been working in that damn barbershop if it wasn't for the shit I did, and Shoney's black ass wouldn't have had half the shit she did had I not given it to her. I knew better, but by the way things were looking, one of them had to have said something to somebody. And by the way they were brushing me off and acting as if they didn't know what was going on, it was as if they thought I was setting them up. All I needed was for either one of them to contact my boy and get me a front. I had spots that were about to dry up, and money was being lost.

Something Brent said stayed at the top of my mind, and when thinking about it, I couldn't help but think about some of the things Shoney said, and the way she was during our most recent visit. Why would they think I was trying to set them up? Where would that thought even come from? I knew I was facing some major shit, but I had never, ever thought about selling out my own people. By the time I made it back to my housing area, I'd come to the conclusion that I was about to sell some items. I'd let the shit die down and hopefully retain a good appeals attorney to represent me. By then, things would have gone back to normal, and all this paranoid shit would be in the rearview mirror. One thing I had to do now was retrace my steps and cover the tracks they had not yet found. I had to call Asia.

***

Brent

With everything happening so fast and money being spent faster, I literally had to pull back and look at things from a distance. Daxx was facing a couple of capital murder counts, and Raylon was looking at conspiracy charges himself. They both needed me to do something for them in one way or the other. Daxx was insisting that I find Sheila and get his money, and that was understood, but Raylon was on some more shit. Not only did I have to frown at the conversations we'd been having, but the nigga continued to call my personal and business phones talking about this when he shouldn't have, and that had me thinking there was a possibility that I was being set up. I wasn't the one to accuse my closest friends of some shit like that, but damn. Raylon was making it hard for me to believe anything else.

Raylon had called me earlier this morning, but because I had things to do, I sent it to voicemail. And seeing that I couldn't be reached at either of the shops, he continually called my cell. Something told me to ignore him, but you know how that went. I reluctantly answered, and from beginning to end, I was either acting as if I didn't know what he was talking about, or was questioning the things he was asking.

"One trip, Brent. That's all I need, man."

"One trip where, Raylon? What are you talking about?" I asked. Shoney had already told me about some of the things he was demanding and accusing her of, and I wasn't about to go there with him.

"Listen, Brent, these—"

"Why you keep saying my name like that, nigga?"

"Will you be quiet and listen? These motherfuckers coming at me with everything. They got wire taps, surveillance, and names. I need for you to get at—"

"This shit don't end like this for me, Raylon. Whatever you got going on ain't some shit I'm trying to get involved with."

"What the fuck is that supposed to mean, nigga?"

"You sitting here asking me to do some shit I don't know anything about. How I know you ain't trying to put me on the cross to get yourself out?"

"Nigga, if I was trying to do some shit like that, you would have been locked up by now."

I knew those words held weight, but it was something that needed to be said. "Y'all my niggas, and I'm going to be there for you, but that's as far as that shit goes, man. All that other stuff you're talking about, I don't know anything about. And if y'all can't respect that then, hey?"

"So this is how y'all going to play it? You and Shoney cutting a nigga off now? After all the shit I've done for y'all?"

"I got to take a call, Raylon. I'll be down to visit you tomorrow," I lied.

The guilt trip wasn't going to work on me the way it worked on Shoney. I might have told Shoney not to do this or that when it came to his request, but it was only said as a means of looking out for her best interest. Sept and I both knew how hard it was for Shoney not to be able to do what Raylon asked, but if she wanted to stay out of prison herself, then there was a line even she had to draw. There was no need in all of us sinking with a ship that was damn near under the waters already, and I'd promised myself a long time ago that my story wasn't about to end that way.

***

Shoney

For the past month or so, I was either going into somebody's courthouse, talking to lawyers, or visiting Raylon, and each time, I prayed I wasn't apprehended for something. Sept was still changing the subject when I brought up our old co-worker, Alyssa, and that had me thinking the worst. She claimed the manager had come to her, but after hearing that she'd quit, and, all of a sudden, moved out of town, I couldn't help but wonder if Sept really had something done to her. All I knew was that without Alyssa's testimony, Sept's case would get dropped, and that was the reason we were at the federal building now. This was the second hearing, and the one I prayed things would eventually lead to all charges being dropped against my girl.

"Between you and Raylon, I don't know who's brought me here the most, Sept," I told her as we walked through the lobby and towards the elevator.

"Don't act like you ain't been charged with some kind of crime, Shoney. If I recall correctly, your black ass dun been to several hearings yourself."

"I'll be glad when all of this mess is behind us. I'm serious. Every time I walk into one of these buildings, I can't help but feel that someone is going to call my name and drag me somewhere I won't come back from," I told her while we waited for the elevator.

"If you do that shit Raylon's begging you to do, you just might end up in some cell, but as long as you stick with me, we'll be in and out of these buildings in no time."

I watched Sept as she removed her glasses and folded them into her purse. The woman just wouldn't stop. These types of settings were her stage, and when I tell you the woman performed at each of them, I mean that literally. We both watched the coming and going of some of everybody, but what caught my attention was when I saw a light-complected woman wearing the exact same boots Raylon bought me just months ago. She was the same chick he'd taken to the new jazz spot I went to with September. Being that I was there for a hearing already, I only shook my head and looked off. I couldn't believe that Raylon had bought me some shit he'd bought another bitch.

"Shoney, this bitch got on your boots," Sept nodded.

"Fuck her, Sept. We have other shit to worry about right now," I told her, not wanting to fuel the already lit fire under her.

"And that bitch got that Christopher Cane bag."

Before I could turn and look, Sept stormed off in the direction the light-complected woman was headed. "September!" Knowing that the woman was likely to do or say something that would have the security summoned, I followed her.

"I know this nigga ain't bought this bitch no $16,000 bag, Shoney."

Seeing the familiar handbag, I began to think the same thing. Raylon and I had this talk, and he promised me that he wasn't seeing her anymore—let alone buying her shit he wouldn't even buy me. I followed Sept until the light-complected woman turned a corner and disappeared behind a door.

"Hey, um, excuse me."

I looked from the door to where Sept had walked. She'd flagged down some older white guy wearing jeans, a light-colored shirt, and a cowboy hat. His appearance screamed feds, and I was praying Sept was able to see that also. I walked to where she stopped and waited for the both of us.

"How may I help you, beautiful?"

"That woman you was just talking to. Who is she?" Sept pointed to the door across the hall. The same one the mixed-breed woman entered.

"You talking 'bout Moore? Well, it's Detective Moore now. She just got promoted recently."

"Detective?" Sept and I asked in unison. My mind traveled a thousand miles in a matter of seconds. My husband was fucking off on me with a federal detective. "Detective?" I heard myself ask a second time.

"She's heading up our narcotics division now," he boasted, proud even.

The rest of the conversation he and Sept had became background noise to my thoughts, because not only had Raylon been lying to me about him still seeing her, but she was a fucking federal detective. The bitch was wearing the exact same boots I had in my closet, and on top of that, she'd gotten a $16,000 handbag out of my husband.

"Shoney, will you bring your black ass on?" September pulled me towards the corner we'd rounded, looked at me, and shook her head. "That's how them hoes know everything. That bitch been setting ya stupid ass husband up for the longest."

"What-what are you talking about, Sept?"

"The bitch's name is Asia Moore. She's been working for these motherfuckers for nine years, and she just got promoted to detective. Add the shit up, Shoney. He must have been telling the bitch something, and she turned his ass in so she could get the promotion. I told you a long time ago these bitches out here playing for keeps."

I knew I told Raylon that I wasn't going to visit for a while, but all that had changed now. I was going to ask him about Asia. I was going to ask about the boots and the Christopher Cane bag, and as soon as he denied knowing about either, I was going to let him know that she was a federal detective. I was going to be right there when the look on his face exposed everything he'd been hiding and lying about for years. Like the many times before, Raylon dug himself a hole he had no way out of, and unlike the other times, I wasn't about to lift a finger to help him out.

Epilogue

Shoney

As expected, the lies continued and the promises were made, but neither mattered anymore. I was through with Rayon. Not only did I find out that he'd continued to fuck with Asia throughout our marriage and that he'd been buying her damn near everything he'd bought me, but he'd gotten some sixteen-year-old prostitute in Mexico pregnant. I could have dealt with the fact that Raylon did his dirt, but him having a child with a minor, a prostitute at that, was too damn much. I knew for a fact that Raylon had dealings in Mexico and had been there on more than one occasion, but now I was seeing the reasons why. Luckily for me, I didn't go, because that's where the feds had been following him, and photos were taken of him and some cartel heads. Photos of him hugged up with the young girl were even taken, but let him tell it, nothing happened between them.

The day I caught that pistol case, the cops had been given a tip, and unfortunately, I was the one they found behind the wheel, and the reason I was only given a slap on the hand was because they knew it wasn't mine, and they knew whose it really was. That Asia chick had been working a case against Raylon's bald-headed ass for the longest but could never land anything solid until recently. Daxx had taken over the day-to-day operation and had a couple of guys she wasn't familiar with making the trips instead of Raylon. It was just a matter of time before they caught up with him, and by the way she explained during her testimony, she personally saw Raylon with large amounts of money and drugs.

The best thing that could have happened was when that Cindy chick had our house robbed, because the feds didn't find anything once they did do a search. That also cleared me of any wrongdoing, because I had Sheila put the house in my name. I'd been dun moved out, and since then, and the fact that Asia testified that I had nothing to do with Raylon's drug transactions and didn't know anything about the double life he lived, I was left alone. We both knew they were lies, but, I was glad she told. I might not have liked the shit she'd done, but I had to respect it. She was trying to make something out of her career, and bringing down drug operations was something she felt would help her. Fucking Raylon just allowed her inside of all he had going on, and she used that to her advantage. Like Sept said, these women were playing for keeps, and it was about time I got on that page also.

Raylon was given a federal life sentence for the conspiracy to distribute, as well as forty years state for the possession of over one thousand grams and possession of a felony firearm. Although I told him that I'd be there for him, my shit was packed before the trial. And on top of that, I was filing for a divorce. It was some sad shit, but I wasn't about to put myself through any of it again. That was not part of the plan.

Daxx, on the other hand, knew he wasn't coming back from the hell he put himself in and was found dead in his cell a day before he was to select a jury. There were still unanswered questions when it came to his death.

THE END

Submission Guideline

Submit the first three chapters of your completed manuscript to ldpsubmissions@gmail.com, subject line: Your book's title. The manuscript must be in a .doc file and sent as an attachment. Document should be in Times New Roman, double spaced and in size 12 font. Also, provide your synopsis and full contact information. If sending multiple submissions, they must each be in a separate email.

Have a story but no way to send it electronically? You can still submit to LDP/Ca$h Presents. Send in the first three chapters, written or typed, of your completed manuscript to:

LDP: Submissions Dept
Po Box 944
Stockbridge, Ga 30281

DO NOT send original manuscript. Must be a duplicate.

Provide your synopsis and a cover letter containing your full contact information.

Thanks for considering LDP and Ca$h Presents.

Coming Soon from Lock Down Publications/Ca$h Presents

BOW DOWN TO MY GANGSTA

By **Ca$h**

TORN BETWEEN TWO

By **Coffee**

THE STREETS STAINED MY SOUL **II**

By **Marcellus Allen**

BLOOD OF A BOSS **VI**

SHADOWS OF THE GAME II

TRAP BASTARD II

By **Askari**

LOYAL TO THE GAME **IV**

By **T.J. & Jelissa**

IF LOVING YOU IS WRONG… **III**

By **Jelissa**

TRUE SAVAGE **VIII**

MIDNIGHT CARTEL IV

DOPE BOY MAGIC IV

CITY OF KINGZ III

By **Chris Green**

BLAST FOR ME **III**

A SAVAGE DOPEBOY III

CUTTHROAT MAFIA III

DUFFLE BAG CARTEL VI

HEARTLESS GOON VI

By **Ghost**

A HUSTLER'S DECEIT III

KILL ZONE **II**

BAE BELONGS TO ME III

A DOPE BOY'S QUEEN III

By **Aryanna**

COKE KINGS V

KING OF THE TRAP II

By **T.J. Edwards**

GORILLAZ IN THE BAY V

3X KRAZY III

De'Kari

THE STREETS ARE CALLING II

Duquie Wilson

KINGPIN KILLAZ IV

STREET KINGS III

PAID IN BLOOD III

CARTEL KILLAZ IV

DOPE GODS III

Hood Rich

SINS OF A HUSTLA II

ASAD

KINGZ OF THE GAME VI

Playa Ray

SLAUGHTER GANG IV

RUTHLESS HEART IV

By Willie Slaughter

FUK SHYT II

By Blakk Diamond

TRAP QUEEN

By Troublesome

YAYO V

GHOST MOB II

Stilloan Robinson

KINGPIN DREAMS III

By Paper Boi Rari

CREAM II

By Yolanda Moore

SON OF A DOPE FIEND III

By Renta

FOREVER GANGSTA II

GLOCKS ON SATIN SHEETS III

By Adrian Dulan

LOYALTY AIN'T PROMISED III

By Keith Williams

THE PRICE YOU PAY FOR LOVE III

By Destiny Skai

I'M NOTHING WITHOUT HIS LOVE II

SINS OF A THUG II

By Monet Dragun

LIFE OF A SAVAGE IV

MURDA SEASON IV

GANGLAND CARTEL IV

CHI'RAQ GANGSTAS IV

KILLERS ON ELM STREET II

By **Romell Tukes**

QUIET MONEY IV

EXTENDED CLIP III

By **Trai'Quan**

THE STREETS MADE ME III

By **Larry D. Wright**

IF YOU CROSS ME ONCE II

ANGEL III

By **Anthony Fields**

FRIEND OR FOE III

By **Mimi**

SAVAGE STORMS III

By **Meesha**

BLOOD ON THE MONEY III

By J-Blunt

THE STREETS WILL NEVER CLOSE II

By K'ajji

NIGHTMARES OF A HUSTLA III

By King Dream

IN THE ARM OF HIS BOSS

By Jamila

MONEY, MURDER & MEMORIES III

Malik D. Rice

CONCRETE KILLAZ II

By Kingpen

HARD AND RUTHLESS II

By Von Wiley Hall

LEVELS TO THIS SHYT II

By Ah'Million

MOB TIES II

By SayNoMore

BODYMORE MURDERLAND II

By Delmont Player

THE LAST OF THE OGS II

Tranay Adams

FOR THE LOVE OF A BOSS II

By C. D. Blue

Available Now

RESTRAINING ORDER **I & II**

By **CA$H & Coffee**

LOVE KNOWS NO BOUNDARIES **I II & III**

By **Coffee**

RAISED AS A GOON I, II, III & IV

BRED BY THE SLUMS I, II, III

BLAST FOR ME I & II

ROTTEN TO THE CORE I II III

A BRONX TALE I, II, III

DUFFLE BAG CARTEL I II III IV V

HEARTLESS GOON I II III IV V

A SAVAGE DOPEBOY I II

DRUG LORDS I II III

CUTTHROAT MAFIA I II

By **Ghost**

LAY IT DOWN **I & II**

LAST OF A DYING BREED I II

BLOOD STAINS OF A SHOTTA I & II III

By **Jamaica**

LOYAL TO THE GAME I II III

LIFE OF SIN I, II III

By **TJ & Jelissa**

BLOODY COMMAS I & II

SKI MASK CARTEL I II & III

KING OF NEW YORK I II,III IV V

RISE TO POWER I II III

COKE KINGS I II III IV

BORN HEARTLESS I II III IV

KING OF THE TRAP

By **T.J. Edwards**

IF LOVING HIM IS WRONG…I & II

LOVE ME EVEN WHEN IT HURTS I II III

By **Jelissa**

WHEN THE STREETS CLAP BACK I & II III

THE HEART OF A SAVAGE I II III

By **Jibril Williams**

A DISTINGUISHED THUG STOLE MY HEART I II & III

LOVE SHOULDN'T HURT I II III IV

RENEGADE BOYS I II III IV

PAID IN KARMA I II III

SAVAGE STORMS I II

By **Meesha**

A GANGSTER'S CODE I &, II III

A GANGSTER'S SYN I II III

THE SAVAGE LIFE I II III

CHAINED TO THE STREETS I II III

BLOOD ON THE MONEY I II

By J-Blunt

PUSH IT TO THE LIMIT

By **Bre' Hayes**

BLOOD OF A BOSS **I, II, III, IV, V**

SHADOWS OF THE GAME

TRAP BASTARD

By **Askari**

THE STREETS BLEED MURDER **I, II & III**

THE HEART OF A GANGSTA I II& III

By **Jerry Jackson**

CUM FOR ME I II III IV V VI

An **LDP Erotica Collaboration**

BRIDE OF A HUSTLA **I II & II**

THE FETTI GIRLS **I, II& III**

CORRUPTED BY A GANGSTA I, II III, IV

BLINDED BY HIS LOVE

THE PRICE YOU PAY FOR LOVE I II

DOPE GIRL MAGIC I II III

By **Destiny Skai**

WHEN A GOOD GIRL GOES BAD

By **Adrienne**

THE COST OF LOYALTY I II III

By Kweli

A GANGSTER'S REVENGE **I II III & IV**

THE BOSS MAN'S DAUGHTERS I II III IV V

A SAVAGE LOVE **I & II**

BAE BELONGS TO ME I II

A HUSTLER'S DECEIT I, II, III

WHAT BAD BITCHES DO I, II, III

SOUL OF A MONSTER I II III

KILL ZONE

A DOPE BOY'S QUEEN I II

By **Aryanna**

A KINGPIN'S AMBITON

A KINGPIN'S AMBITION **II**

I MURDER FOR THE DOUGH

By **Ambitious**

TRUE SAVAGE I II III IV V VI VII

DOPE BOY MAGIC I, II, III

MIDNIGHT CARTEL I II III

CITY OF KINGZ I II

By **Chris Green**

A DOPEBOY'S PRAYER

By **Eddie "Wolf" Lee**

THE KING CARTEL **I, II & III**

By **Frank Gresham**

THESE NIGGAS AIN'T LOYAL **I, II & III**

By **Nikki Tee**

GANGSTA SHYT **I II &III**

By **CATO**

THE ULTIMATE BETRAYAL

By **Phoenix**

BOSS'N UP **I , II & III**

By **Royal Nicole**

I LOVE YOU TO DEATH

By Destiny J

I RIDE FOR MY HITTA

I STILL RIDE FOR MY HITTA

By **Misty Holt**

LOVE & CHASIN' PAPER

By **Qay Crockett**

TO DIE IN VAIN

SINS OF A HUSTLA

By **ASAD**

BROOKLYN HUSTLAZ

By **Boogsy Morina**

BROOKLYN ON LOCK I & II

By **Sonovia**

GANGSTA CITY

By **Teddy Duke**

A DRUG KING AND HIS DIAMOND I & II III

A DOPEMAN'S RICHES

HER MAN, MINE'S TOO I, II

CASH MONEY HO'S

THE WIFEY I USED TO BE I II

By Nicole Goosby

TRAPHOUSE KING **I II & III**

KINGPIN KILLAZ I II III

STREET KINGS I II

PAID IN BLOOD **I II**

CARTEL KILLAZ I II III

DOPE GODS I II

By **Hood Rich**

LIPSTICK KILLAH **I, II, III**

CRIME OF PASSION I II & III

FRIEND OR FOE I II

By **Mimi**

STEADY MOBBN' **I, II, III**

THE STREETS STAINED MY SOUL

By **Marcellus Allen**

WHO SHOT YA **I, II, III**

SON OF A DOPE FIEND I II

Renta

GORILLAZ IN THE BAY **I II III IV**

TEARS OF A GANGSTA I II

3X KRAZY I II

DE'KARI

TRIGGADALE I II III

Elijah R. Freeman

GOD BLESS THE TRAPPERS I, II, III

THESE SCANDALOUS STREETS I, II, III

FEAR MY GANGSTA I, II, III IV, V

THESE STREETS DON'T LOVE NOBODY I, II

BURY ME A G I, II, III, IV, V

A GANGSTA'S EMPIRE I, II, III, IV

THE DOPEMAN'S BODYGAURD I II

THE REALEST KILLAZ I II III

THE LAST OF THE OGS

Tranay Adams

THE STREETS ARE CALLING

Duquie Wilson

MARRIED TO A BOSS… I II III

By Destiny Skai & Chris Green

KINGZ OF THE GAME I II III IV V

Playa Ray

SLAUGHTER GANG I II III

RUTHLESS HEART I II III

By Willie Slaughter

FUK SHYT

By Blakk Diamond

DON'T F#CK WITH MY HEART I II

By Linnea

ADDICTED TO THE DRAMA I II III

IN THE ARM OF HIS BOSS II

By Jamila

YAYO I II III IV

A SHOOTER'S AMBITION I II

By S. Allen

TRAP GOD I II III

By Troublesome

FOREVER GANGSTA

GLOCKS ON SATIN SHEETS I II

By Adrian Dulan

TOE TAGZ I II III

LEVELS TO THIS SHYT

By Ah'Million

KINGPIN DREAMS I II

By Paper Boi Rari

CONFESSIONS OF A GANGSTA I II III

By Nicholas Lock

I'M NOTHING WITHOUT HIS LOVE

SINS OF A THUG

By Monet Dragun

CAUGHT UP IN THE LIFE I II III

By Robert Baptiste

NEW TO THE GAME I II III

MONEY, MURDER & MEMORIES I II

By **Malik D. Rice**

LIFE OF A SAVAGE I II III

A GANGSTA'S QUR'AN I II III

MURDA SEASON I II III

GANGLAND CARTEL I II III

CHI'RAQ GANGSTAS I II III

KILLERS ON ELM STREET

By **Romell Tukes**

LOYALTY AIN'T PROMISED I II

By Keith Williams

QUIET MONEY I II III

THUG LIFE I II

EXTENDED CLIP I II

By **Trai'Quan**

THE STREETS MADE ME I II

By **Larry D. Wright**

THE ULTIMATE SACRIFICE I, II, III, IV, V, VI

KHADIFI

IF YOU CROSS ME ONCE

ANGEL I II

By **Anthony Fields**

THE LIFE OF A HOOD STAR

By Ca$h & Rashia Wilson

THE STREETS WILL NEVER CLOSE

By K'ajji

CREAM

By Yolanda Moore

NIGHTMARES OF A HUSTLA I II

By King Dream

CONCRETE KILLAZ

By Kingpen

HARD AND RUTHLESS

By Von Wiley Hall

GHOST MOB II

Stilloan Robinson

MOB TIES

By SayNoMore

BODYMORE MURDERLAND

By Delmont Player

FOR THE LOVE OF A BOSS

By C. D. Blue

BOOKS BY LDP'S CEO, CA$H

TRUST IN NO MAN

TRUST IN NO MAN 2

TRUST IN NO MAN 3

BONDED BY BLOOD

SHORTY GOT A THUG

THUGS CRY

THUGS CRY 2

THUGS CRY 3

TRUST NO BITCH

TRUST NO BITCH 2

TRUST NO BITCH 3

TIL MY CASKET DROPS

RESTRAINING ORDER

RESTRAINING ORDER 2

IN LOVE WITH A CONVICT

LIFE OF A HOOD STAR

CPSIA information can be obtained
at www.ICGtesting.com
Printed in the USA
LVHW080728060821
694541LV00023B/927